D1269715

"A heartfelt tale filled with whimsy, wonder, and magic . . . **truly satisfying.**"

—*Publishers Weekly*, **starred review**

"Funny, compassionate, and entertaining . . .
Readers will be immersed into this dark yet humorous world filled with unique characters."

—*School Library Journal*

"Intruders in the dungeon! A **lighthearted fantasy** with a strong start."

—*Kirkus*

"A **fun and creative** story with **surprisingly deep plot twists.**"

—*Booklist*

A Junior Library Guild Selection

PRAISE FOR

"This action-packed, fast-paced read is funny, heartfelt, and filled with adventure."

—*School Library Journal: Xpress Reviews*

VOYAGE ON THE EVERSTEEL SEA

ADAM JAY EPSTEIN

[Imprint]
MAKE YOUR MARK

New York

[Imprint]
MAKE YOUR MARK

A part of Macmillan Publishing Group, LLC
120 Broadway, New York, NY 10271

SNARED: VOYAGE ON THE EVERSTEEL SEA.
Copyright © 2020 by Adam Jay Epstein. All rights reserved.
Printed in the United States of America by
LSC Communications, Harrisonburg, Virginia.

Library of Congress Cataloging-in-Publication Data is available.

ISBN 978-1-250-14697-7 (hardcover) / ISBN 978-1-250-14696-0 (ebook)

Our books may be purchased in bulk for promotional, educational, or business
use. Please contact your local bookseller or the Macmillan Corporate and
Premium Sales Department at (800) 221-7945 ext. 5442 or by email
at MacmillanSpecialMarkets@macmillan.com.

Book design by Eileen Savage

Imprint logo designed by Amanda Spielman

First edition, 2020

1   3   5   7   9   10   8   6   4   2

mackids.com

If you've slipped this book into your everstuff sack,
I would strongly advise that you put it right back.
Or you just might spend your life in Carrion Tomb,
Never again to see your above-ground room.

FOR MY VILLAGE

TABLE OF CONTENTS

1

BLACK SMOKE RISING

A hand grabbed Wily by the shoulder and shook him awake. It was still the middle of the night. The half-moon peeked through the fluttering silk curtains that hung from the wrought iron rods framing his bedroom windows. He rolled over, eager to discover who was standing beside him at this late hour.

He saw no one. He rubbed his eyes and looked again. There was no face looking down at him. Wily felt his shoulder jostled once more. Startled, he tilted his head lower to see that the hand belonged to Righteous, the enchanted hovering arm that had once been firmly attached to the shoulder of the knight Pryvyd.

Something was very wrong. Roveeka, his surrogate hobgoblet sister, might wake him up in the middle of the night if she had a bad dream. His blue-haired friend,

Odette, might tiptoe into his room before dawn if she was feeling extra cheerful and wanted to watch the sunrise from the branches of the apple trees outside the royal palace gates with him. But Righteous would never stir Wily from sleep unless it was a matter of urgent importance.

"What's happening?" Wily said with alarm.

Righteous responded by grabbing Wily's trapsmith belt off the chair and tossing it onto the bed.

Now Wily was certain there was trouble. He quickly strapped on the belt, made sure all its stuffed pouches and tools were still attached to it, and rushed after Righteous, who was already flying out of his bedroom and into the upstairs hall.

Wily's mind raced with possibilities as his bare feet pounded against the smooth stone tiles. *Had the golems returned? Was Stalag attacking the outside walls with a new army of evil minions? Or was it even worse?*

He continued down the hall past the library where he had spent the last six months trying, in vain, to perfect his reading skills. He was starting to feel like he was the only thirteen-year-old in the whole land who still wasn't a master reader. Righteous was knocking on the doors as it flew ahead.

"Are you going off to adventure without me?" Odette said as she bounded out of her room. She was an extremely light sleeper.

"I'm not even sure what's going on," Wily said as she hustled up beside him.

"Mysterious missions in the middle of the night are way better than sleeping," Odette chirped.

Odette was a morning elf, bright and cheerful early in the day, no matter how early it was.

Righteous led them past the tapestries of the old rulers of Panthasos to the high balcony that looked out over the countryside. Wily stopped in his tracks. In the distance beyond Trumpet Pass, he could see black smoke rising from the foot of Mount Neb. Although obscured by the hills between, he knew what stood there: the last of the prisonauts, which now housed the most traitorous and dangerous criminals in the land, including the very worst of them: the former ruler of Panthasos, Kestrel Gromanov, better known as the Infernal King. The cruel king was feared and hated by all, but none more than his son, Wily Snare.

"What are you looking at?" a drowsy voice said from behind them.

Wily turned to see Roveeka rubbing her eyes awake. He pointed into the distance.

"The prisonaut," Wily said with dread. "Can you see the smoke?"

"That's not good," Roveeka said, still disoriented. "They're having a midnight barbecue without us."

"I think it might be a little more serious than that,"

Odette said as Wily stepped out onto the balcony, where Righteous was now floating.

Wily looked over the edge to see that Pryvyd was on his horse alongside a dozen Knights of the Golden Sun, their well-polished armor sparkling in the glow of the half-moon's light. Moshul, the mouthless moss golem, stood nearby, a swarm of fireflies buzzing around his head. The knights and golem appeared ready for travel.

"Do you know what happened?" Wily shouted down to Pryvyd.

"The prisonaut's outer wall was blasted open," Pryvyd replied. "All the cavern mages and oglodytes that marched with Stalag are escaping."

"That's right," a young prison guard said. "We need help. There's too many prisoners for us to handle on our own. They're not going to let themselves get recaptured without a fight."

"And my father?" Wily said with rising concern. "Did he escape too?"

"That's what we're going to find out," Pryvyd said with a very worried look. "Hurry down! If they get too far, we'll never find them."

"Moshul!" Odette shouted to get the moss golem's attention. She then made a series of quick hand gestures. Wily was getting better at translating sign language. He had been training himself in the silent form of communication so that he could understand what Moshul was saying without Odette or Pryvyd having to translate for him. If he was correct, Odette had just signed "Catch me."

Wily's eyes went wide as Odette took a few steps back and sprinted for the stone railing that encircled the balcony. With a front handspring off the railing, Odette soared out into the air. She somersaulted three times before landing in Moshul's waiting arms.

"Come on, Wily," Odette shouted. "You're next. It's a thrill."

"Wait!" Pryvyd yelled. "If your mother knew I let you jump off the parapets, she'd kill me."

"She's off replanting the Twighast Forest with Valor and the other Roamabouts," Odette said. "She'll never know."

"Well, I don't know how comfortable I am with it either," added Pryvyd as he surveyed the drop.

"Now you're sounding like a concerned parent," Odette teased.

Pryvyd seemed conflicted. Then, seeming as if he didn't really want to, he shouted: "Come on already!"

Wily sprinted for the edge and jumped. He hoped dearly that he wasn't making a very big mistake. He dropped through the air and into Moshul's mossy fingers.

Roveeka cupped her hands around her mouth and shouted down to Wily.

"Go without me!" the hobgoblet said. "I have to go to the kitchen first."

"I love her," Odette said to Wily, "but sometimes she thinks too much with her stomach."

As HIS HORSE'S hooves pounded against the gravel path, Wily thought about the last time he had visited with his father. He had gone to him with questions about a statue that had been stolen from Stilt Village, one that had turned out to be a key part in Stalag's plan to find enough neccanite to build an enormous unbreakable golem. During that discussion, his father had tried to escape, and it was through sheer luck that he had been prevented from doing so. Tonight, they might not be so lucky again.

Coming around a bend in the path, Wily spied a thick plume of smoke rising from a giant hole in the steel wall of the prisonaut. The imposing structure had once rolled around Panthasos on giant wheels, but they had been removed after the Infernal King was dethroned. Since then, it had remained there, a dirt-swept relic of the evil reign that came before. But now it looked sadder still. The damage to the prisonaut was worse than Wily had imagined. Ribbons of metal lay scattered across the mountainside as fires burned within. The sounds of swords clashing were echoing in the darkness.

"Only the spiked tail of Palojax, the great lair beast, is capable of this level of destruction," Odette said as she rode alongside Wily.

"Or the spell of a very powerful cavern mage," Wily said. "Or more likely many cavern mages working together."

"Knights of the Golden Sun," a shrill voice called out in panic.

Wily turned to the left, in the direction of the voice, to see a mob of figures running past. Even in the dim glow of the moonlight, he could see they were fish-headed oglodytes sprinting away from the prisonaut.

"Run for the river," one of the web-handed escapees shouted to his companions.

"Don't let those oglodytes get to water!" Pryvyd called out. "Otherwise, we'll never recapture them."

"We're on it, Captain," a knight called out as she pulled a weighted net from the satchel strapped to the side of her horse.

Pryvyd and his fellow Knights of the Golden Sun turned their mounts to intercept the oglodytes. They stretched their nets between the galloping mares to scoop up the fleeing fish-folk. Wily watched as the first oglodyte was snared in the ropes and began flopping around like a tunnel trout pulled from an underground stream.

"Keep heading for the prisonaut," Pryvyd shouted to Wily. "Let us handle this bunch."

As the knights continued their pursuit of the oglodytes, Wily, Odette, and Moshul charged through a maze of boulders toward the hole in the wall of the prisonaut. Wily gave his horse a nudge to speed her along. He could see more prisoners flooding out of the steel structure. He only hoped that his father was not one of them.

"Look out!" Odette yelled.

A drooling slither troll sprang from behind a boulder and pounced onto the back of Wily's horse. He dug his long claws into Wily's shirt.

"This horse is mine now," the slither troll said as he lifted Wily over his head and tossed him from the saddle. Wily went tumbling through the air before landing with a crash on the ground. He watched as the slither troll galloped off with his horse. A careless mistake. Wily wondered how he could have been so foolish.

Five more slither trolls bounded out from behind the rocks, swiping the air menacingly with their black claws. Clear liquid oozed from the hideous creatures' skin and out of their long, crooked noses.

"I want a pony too," one of the trolls said as he tried to tackle the legs of Odette's mount.

"Sweet, slime-coated revenge," a deep voice chortled from nearby.

Wily looked up from the hard earth to see a rotund cavern mage floating a few feet off the ground. He had met this unpleasant character before, in the arid plain of the Parchlands: Girthbellow was one of the cavern mages who had joined Stalag in his quest to build a stone golem army that could take over Panthasos. Now the mage watched with delight as a trio of slither trolls jumped onto Moshul and began biting the moss golem.

"Oh yes!" Girthbellow shouted as he hovered above the earth. "I am enjoying this."

"Were you the one responsible for this prison break?" Wily called out.

"Not I," Girthbellow replied. "But I certainly plan on taking full advantage of it."

Girthbellow raised his hand, causing a nearby rock to rise off the ground and levitate next to him.

"This stone is very heavy," he said with mock concern. "My enchantment can barely hold it up."

He thrust out his hand, sending the rock flying forward. It moved through the air, heading straight for Wily.

"Oh dear, I think I might have to drop it," Girthbellow chuckled. "And make some smashed prince preserves. My slither trolls would enjoy eating that on toast."

Wily rolled out of the way, trying to keep himself out from under the shadow of the hovering boulder.

"No tomatoes to save you this time," Girthbellow announced delightedly.

During their last encounter, Wily had constructed a slingshot to fire mildly acidic tomatoes at the sensitive-skinned slither trolls. It had been a smashing success, but it had turned Wily off tomatoes permanently.

The boulder was closing in on Wily when, seemingly out of nowhere, a knife soared through the air, hitting the back of Girthbellow's hand. The impact interrupted the cavern mage's spell, causing the boulder to drop to the ground right next to Wily's feet.

"But he has something better than tomatoes." Roveeka's voice could be heard from beyond the boulders. "He's got a band of angry hobgoblet chefs!"

This was followed by a chorus of voices excitedly shouting, "Grand Slouch! Grand Slouch! Grand Slouch!"

To Wily's delight, dozens of hobgoblets came riding into view, three to a horse. Since Roveeka had discovered that the entire hobgoblet society was tricked by humans into living in the Below centuries ago, Wily and the Kingdom of Panthasos had tried to make amends by inviting the hobgoblets back to the Above. Some of them had ended up working in the palace kitchen, a place most suited to their amazing knife-wielding and unique culinary skills, while others had spread across the kingdom to start their own restaurants and mushroom farms. Wily realized that Roveeka had not been going to the palace kitchen to get a snack; she had been recruiting a small, wart-skinned army.

The droopy-eyed band of apron-wearing hobgoblets flew off their horses and onto the backs of the trolls. What ensued was a chaos of biting and poking.

"Keep fighting, my friends from the Below!" Roveeka called out.

Girthbellow realized that the odds of a quick victory were no longer in his favor. The cavern mage spun around in the air and began to hover off.

"Not so fast," Odette called out as she grabbed a fistful of yellow mushrooms from Moshul's shoulders.

She flung them at the ground beneath Girthbellow. The mushrooms exploded into a cloud of yellow smoke. The cavern mage coughed once before dropping to the ground like a confused bat that had smacked its head into a stalactite.

As the hobgoblets continued their assault, Wily got back to his feet and snagged a loose horse. He had no time for celebration. He had a more urgent purpose. He snapped the reins of the horse and raced for the prisonaut.

Getting closer, Wily could see guards, injured and coughing, come stumbling out of the smoke. The horse that he was riding, frightened by the flames, skidded to a halt with a fearful whinny. Wily dropped from the back of his mount and sprinted for the destroyed wall.

"Turn back, Wily," a guard said, grabbing him by the wrist. "It's not safe in there."

But Wily ignored his plea. He twisted his arm free and ran through the shredded wall, leaping shards of steel that had melted into pools of liquid metal.

Once inside the courtyard of the prisonaut, Wily discovered guards in sword fights with wild-eyed boarcus. A few of the cottages were burning, with thick layers of smoke rising from the wooden ceiling beams. There were many prisonaut guards in need of assistance, but before he could help them, Wily had to make sure that the biggest threat to the land was still in shackles.

He ran past the prisonaut's center fountain to the cottage that housed the most dangerous prisoner. He had been there before. He knew which one was his father's. His eyes trained on a thatched-roof cottage with black outer walls.

He could see that the door to his father's prison cottage was open, swinging loosely on its hinges, and his heart skipped a beat. He sprinted for it, fear building inside him. Pushing past the wooden door, he found himself in a room with a single bed and a chair. The cottage appeared empty. His father had escaped.

2

CLUES ON THE GROUND

Wily was about to turn and run back for the door when he heard something move under the bed. He quickly reached into one of his pouches, searching for an object with which to defend himself. He pulled out a small bronze wrench. He suddenly felt very foolish for having come into a prison cottage alone and unarmed during a breakout. His father could have a sword or a knife or an arrow. What good would a wrench do against those? Despite his doubts, he held the metal tool aloft as threateningly as he could.

"I won't let you get past me," Wily said with his boldest air of confidence.

"Weez don't want any trouble," a trembling voice said.

"We just want to be left alone-ish," a second voice chimed in.

This was not what Wily had been expecting. Neither voice belonged to his calculating and eloquent father. Instead, these were the voices of Agorop and Sceely, the oglodytes he had spent countless meals sitting across from during his childhood in Carrion Tomb.

Wily pulled up the bedsheet to reveal the two oglodytes cowering underneath.

"We learned our lesson," Agorop said. "We isn't goin a mess with you no more."

"What are you doing in here?" Wily asked, not trusting the two, who were well-known for telling lies. "This is my father's prison cottage."

"The door was open," Sceely explained. "We came in here to avoid the battle outshide. Most of the other prisoners aren't as delight-ar-i-fic and friendly as us."

"Where's my father?" Wily asked. "The Infernal King?"

"Beats us," Agorop said, shrugging.

"How's would we know?" Sceely said.

"But we will help you as much as we can," Agorop said as he placed both of his webbed hands before Wily's feet as if worshipping him. Sceely did the same.

"I must have missed something," Pryvyd said, entering the cottage to witness this strange scene. "Where's Kestrel?"

"Not here," Wily said as Odette and Roveeka pushed inside, past Pryvyd.

"Well, if it isn't you two again," Odette said with a sigh as she eyed the two oglodytes.

"We're on your side now," Sceely said. "We don't want any more trouble."

Odette reached into her new everstuff satchel and pulled out a pair of enchanted shackles.

"Then you won't mind putting on these," Odette said as she approached the two oglodytes.

"Not at all," Sceely said.

"I'm sure they will be very comfor-it-able!" Agorop said.

"Tell us everything you saw," Odette said as she snapped the shackles around their wrists.

The two oglodytes began to ramble, talking over each other, interrupting and finishing each other's sentences. They recounted how they had been in their own prison cottage eating scraps they had saved from dinner when the sound of a giant explosion shook the prisonaut.

"It must have been the most powerful spell there has ever been," Sceely said. "It shook the walls like a dozen lightning bolts striking all at once."

"I was so frightened that I nearly swallowed the lizard toe I had been munching on," Agorop stammered.

They continued to ramble about how a figure draped in cloaks unlocked their cottage and how they were too scared to escape with all the guards racing through the courtyard. In truth, they were saying very little that was helpful. They were wasting precious time.

Wily hurried out into the prison courtyard again, where Pryvyd was now barking orders to the knights, who were putting out the fires burning in the cottages near the hole in the wall.

"As soon as you're done," Pryvyd shouted, "I want you to search every corner of the prisonaut for Kestrel. And if you don't find him inside, start making circles around the outside perimeter."

Meanwhile, other knights and prison guards were leading those escapees who had been caught back through the gates into the courtyard. Oglodytes tangled in rope nets struggled as they were dragged to their cottages. Cavern mages, shackled with enchanted chains to keep them from using their magic, walked in a single-file line toward their extra-secure cells. Moshul carried the still unconscious Girthbellow in his hands. Wily knew that these were only a small portion of the prisonaut's inhabitants. He wondered just how many had escaped into the night and how long it would take to find them all again. Yet there was only one who truly mattered: his father.

As Pryvyd continued to manage the return of the captives, Wily decided to do some investigating on his own. He wanted to see if there was any evidence that could point to the kind of spell used in the attack on the prisonaut and if that spell had been cast from the inside or the outside. He walked to the spot where the wall had been blown through and began looking for the powdery residue that was a surefire clue to a spell having been cast. He could remember the hundreds of times he had had to clean up the leftover dust from Stalag's spells in Carrion Tomb. The only good thing about the chore was that it wasn't as difficult or sticky a mess as mopping slug slime. A wet rag would do the trick.

As Wily bent over to examine a portion of the ground, a furry hand shot out from a pile of rubble and grabbed him by the wrist.

"I got the prince," a boarcus said as he held tight to Wily's arm.

Wily had been distracted and so hadn't noticed the tusk-faced dungeon dweller hiding just an arm's length away. He tried to reach for his trapsmith belt, but the boarcus grabbed his other wrist before he could. The unpleasant creature pinned both of Wily's hands behind his back and then wrapped his other arm around Wily's neck.

"In exchange for his life," the boarcus screamed, "I want my freedom and a thousand gold pieces from the—"

He never finished his demand. The blunt end of a knife clunked him in the forehead. The boarcus dropped to the ground, his furry hand releasing Wily's wrists and his arm sliding off his neck. Wily picked up the knife from the ground. He only needed to glance at its curved metal blade and its careful etching of a fire-breathing lizard for a moment to know to who this knife belonged.

"Here you go, Roveeka," Wily said as he looked up to see his hobgoblet sister approaching. "Pops hit its target, as always."

Roveeka had two special knives that she kept on her side at all times. She had named them Mum and Pops after the parents she had always wished she had but never did.

"Mum and Pops don't just look out for me," Roveeka said. "They keep you out of trouble too." She took a glance around the spot where Wily was standing as the guards and knights went back to work. "What are you doing over here by all the wreckage?"

"Trying to figure out what kind of spell blew up this wall."

As Wily continued to scan the area around the destroyed wall, he saw no signs of spell residue. He did find something else though: gears, metal sprockets, and screws. These were not things used to cast spells. They were what was used to make machines. Looking farther, he found a small pile of singed firebat guano.

"Look what I found," Wily said to Roveeka.

"Bat droppings?" Roveeka asked. "What are they doing here?"

Wily leaned down and picked up a handful of the crumbly material. Then he took a whiff. The guano smelled as if it had just been cooked in a fire.

"Do you think someone was making a bonfire to toast slugs?" Roveeka asked aloud.

In Carrion Tomb, bat guano was used for two things. One was certainly for building bonfires for the hobgoblets and oglodytes after successfully keeping invaders at bay. The other time Wily had used this combustible substance was in the flame flingers to help ignite the traps. It was extremely explosive when lit.

"It wasn't magic that was at work here," Wily said to Roveeka as he sprinkled the burnt ash in her hand. "This was the doing of a machine. I think my father built something to cause this explosion."

"Impossible," a nearby guard who must have overheard Wily said. "We ensured that he had no tools. Not even one. I think we can all agree it is impossible to build anything without the proper tools."

"I agree," Wily said. "Without tools, it would be very difficult to build a machine that could do this."

Wily's eyes fell on a nearby pile of rubble where he saw something very familiar catching the light of the moon. Under a piece of fallen steel wall, a brown wooden handle with a thin metal neck stuck out. He walked over to the object and pulled it free.

During Wily's previous trip to the prisonaut, his father had stolen a screwdriver from his belt. His father had been caught before he could get far, but the screwdriver was never found. Now Wily was looking down at that very same screwdriver in his hand. *Could it have played a part in the prison break? Had my mistake months earlier caused all this?*

Moshul, Pryvyd, Righteous, and Odette walked up to Wily, who held the screwdriver in his open palms.

"This is mine," Wily said, sorrow in his voice. "My father was responsible for this explosion. There's no question of that now." He hooked the screwdriver back onto his trapsmith belt.

"Don't blame yourself," Odette said. "It was a mistake."

"A very big one," he said.

Wily had learned the hard way that princes didn't need to be perfect, but were they allowed to make kingdom-threatening mistakes such as this one? Did he really deserve another chance after this error? He wasn't so sure.

"He couldn't have made it far yet," Pryvyd said. "We'll find him." The knight led Wily, Odette, Roveeka, Righteous, and Moshul out through the blasted hole in the prisonaut's wall. Roveeka still had her nose buried deep in the handful of bat guano. The others were looking at her strangely.

"It's a very calming smell," she said with a crooked smile. "I used to burn flecks of it in my sleeping chamber to help me fall asleep."

"Bat droppings?" Odette asked, obviously disgusted.

"Why? What kind of droppings did you use?"

"Keep your eyes down," Pryvyd added. "Hopefully, we can track his footprints."

Moshul sent out a swarm of fireflies to light the ground. As the earth was illuminated, Wily did not see a pair of footprints . . . rather he saw thousands of them. They went in every direction and were of all shapes and sizes.

"Easier said than done," Odette said as she scanned her surroundings. "How can we possibly know which footprints are his?"

"What is it, Moshul?" Roveeka asked the moss golem, who had come up beside her. He was signing something with excitement as two types of flies buzzed around Roveeka's head, Moshul's mossy fingers moving through the air in a blur of gestures. Wily didn't catch any of the words.

"Slow down," Wily said.

Moshul repeated the motions slower and bigger for Wily's and the others' benefit. Pryvyd began translating for him.

"His rot flies," Pryvyd said, gesturing to some large gray gnats, "love the smell of the bat droppings even more than Roveeka does."

"I don't think that's possible," Odette said as she spied Roveeka dabbing the dried powder on her wrist and sniffing it.

"And rot flies can follow a scent for miles," Pryvyd

continued to translate. "All we need to do is follow the flies. There must still be guano on your father."

The rot flies buzzed off to the west, with the entire group in close pursuit.

o○o

As THEY CONTINUED to move, Wily kept his eyes on the ground. The density of the footprints was thinning out. The other escapees of the prisonaut must have fled in different directions. The rot flies zipped along the ground with a throbbing buzz of delight. Soon, the group was following just one pair of footprints. Wily could see they were made by pointy boots, very likely the boots of his father.

With the path laid out before them, Odette was moving swiftly, even outpacing the rot flies. Wily tried to keep up with her.

"Over here," Odette shouted.

Wily rushed to where Odette was waving her arms. She pointed to the ground.

Wily could barely make out anything in the dim glow of the moon, but once Moshul's fireflies surrounded them, Wily could see that the trail of footprints along the dusty ground suddenly disappeared.

"Where did the footsteps go?" Pryvyd asked.

Odette gestured another few feet ahead to a set of parallel lines in the dirt as thick as Moshul's wrists. Wily knew at once what they were.

"Wheel tracks," he said.

"And judging by their thickness," Odette added, "this was no ordinary wagon either. Those look like snagglecart tracks. I didn't realize there were any still left assembled."

Snagglecarts were the rolling cages shaped like dragons that had been used by the Infernal King to snatch up innocent people he wished to capture and imprison. After Kestrel's defeat, Wily had insisted that all the frightening creations of his father were disassembled. Clearly, one had escaped this fate.

"The Infernal King wasn't working alone," Pryvyd said to Wily. "Your father was picked up from this spot by somebody."

Moshul placed his head down on the ground. Like every golem, he could hear vibrations in the earth, which he was made of. The ground could often tell him about things that were happening miles away. Wily hoped dearly that this was one of those times. After a moment, Moshul lifted his head. With a twinkle in his jeweled eyes, he began to sign. Once again, his fingers were moving too fast for Wily to understand. Fortunately, Odette didn't have that problem.

"Moshul hears a rumbling in the distance to the west," Odette said. "He's positive it's the sound of a snagglecart rolling."

"How far away?" Wily asked.

"Ten miles," Moshul signed. "Maybe more."

"We should go now," Wily said. "Before we lose them."

Righteous flew off toward where the horses were standing outside the prisonaut.

"Hold on," Pryvyd said. "Your mom and Valor will want to come on this hunt too."

Wily was already shaking his head. "They're in the Twighast. We don't have time to retrieve them or wait for them to return to the palace. My father is already far ahead of us."

"Valor's and Lumina's skills might be helpful when we confront Kestrel," Pryvyd argued. "I know Lumina would want a part in this."

"You can go back," Wily said, "but I'm not waiting."

"And leave you to deal with the Infernal King and his accomplice on your own?" Pryvyd said with disbelief. "I think not."

"You don't need to take care of Wily," Odette said. "Or me for that matter."

"That's not what I meant."

Righteous came back holding the reins of their horses in hand.

"Then get on your horse and join us," Wily said.

Odette did a running backflip onto her horse. Wily mounted his horse as Pryvyd looked on, conflicted. Roveeka climbed up onto Moshul's back, her usual traveling accommodations.

"We are hardly prepared for a long trip," Pryvyd said, still hesitant.

"You're telling me?" Odette asked. "I'm still wearing my pajama bottoms. At least you have a suit of armor on."

Wily looked down to remember that he was wearing his nightshirt too. When he had tucked himself into bed six hours earlier, he hadn't planned for the possibility of a late-night adventure. From now on, he would always be sleeping in his shirt and pants.

3

JOUSTING AT THE
DIRTY VAGABOND

"Are you sure," Odette asked Moshul, "you don't hear the rumble of a snagglecart?"

The companions had been traveling for hours, stopping periodically to allow Moshul to check that they were still heading in the right direction. The moss golem once again had the side of his head pressed to the ground, listening carefully. After a longer than normal pause, he signed to the group.

"He hears many other sounds but not a snagglecart," Odette translated. "They must have stopped somewhere to the southwest of here."

"There's nothing between here and Freemont," Pryvyd said, "unless they camped out on the side of the road."

Moshul signed back to Odette and Pryvyd.

"What kind of sounds do you hear?" Odette asked.

This time Wily was able to understand what Moshul signed. He repeated the words aloud. "Many creatures with eight legs."

"Could there be giant scorpions out here?" Roveeka asked.

"Doubtful," Pryvyd said. "They are found mostly to the south."

Odette grinned broadly, as if she had just solved a puzzle.

"I know what those sounds are," she said. "Spider jousting! It must be where the Dirty Vagabond has set up its tent."

"Spider jousting?" Roveeka asked. "The Dirty Vagabond? I've never heard of either of those things."

"Neither have I," Wily said. "And I'm supposed to be the king one day. I should know this kind of stuff."

"It's not exactly castle conversation," Odette said. "The Dirty Vagabond is a festival for the, hmm, let's say the less friendly members of Panthasos. Burglemeisters and bounty hunters need a place to relax as well."

"It's the kind of place your father would be able to recruit a small army if he wished," Pryvyd explained. "Or blend into the background without anyone asking any questions."

"And the spider jousting?" Wily asked.

"Two giant venomous ghost spiders," Odette said, "are ridden by gwarves with blunt axes and then pitted against each other in a vicious battle of survival."

"It sounds horrible," Roveeka said.

"It's actually far worse than my words can describe," Odette said. "You want to go and check it out?"

"If there's a chance my father is there," Wily said, "then yes."

Wily, Pryvyd, and Odette remounted their horses, and Roveeka climbed onto Moshul's back again. Righteous floated at the front of the group as the mighty moss golem led the way.

"After months cooped up in the palace," Odette said, gripping the reins in her hands, "it feels amazing to be out on the hunt again." The dusty wind flapped through her sapphire hair as she leaned forward in her saddle. "And I know we're not out searching for treasure like we did before Wily reclaimed the kingdom, but right now it kind of feels that way."

Before Wily had been pulled out of Carrion Tomb to join them, Odette, Pryvyd, Righteous, and Moshul had been raiding dungeons for treasure in an attempt to collect enough gold to flee Panthasos and the reign of the Infernal King forever. Their plan had been to have Wily aid them in their quest, knowing that his trap-building skills could be used to disarm traps as well. In fact, it had worked once, when they'd explored Squalor Keep and he had saved their lives from a set of crushing walls. Of course, they had never counted on the fact that Wily was much more than the finest trapsmith in the land; he was a prince in waiting.

"Well this 'treasure' we're looking for now," Pryvyd responded, "has a rather nasty habit of removing limbs."

It had been the Infernal King's mechanical suit of armor that had separated Righteous from Pryvyd's shoulder. And that wasn't the only horrible thing that Wily's father had done by far while he ruled Panthasos. Forests had been burned, towns razed, and families torn apart.

"I hate him even more than you do," Odette said. Her parents had lost their lives in one of his prisonauts when she was just a little girl. "Don't forget that I was the one who suggested throwing Kestrel down a bottomless hole."

"Actually," Wily said, thinking back, "I don't recall you ever saying that at all."

"Oh yeah. I might have just mentioned that to Moshul after we captured Kestrel in the Infernal Fortress. But Moshul thought that would be a little inappropriate."

Moshul nodded and signed to the others.

"It would not have made us as bad as him," Odette countered Moshul. "He deserved a very long fall. And a bottomless hole is bottomless, in which case he wouldn't have been hurt. Just trapped forever. Without food. In the dark."

Which was, as Wily and the others knew, not exactly the truth. They had found the bottoms of at least a few so-called bottomless holes in a land far beneath the surface of the earth, known as the Below, during their last adventure. And there was no pile of pillows down there to cushion the blow.

"No one deserves that kind of punishment," Pryvyd said. "Even someone as awful as Kestrel Gromanov."

"Have you already forgotten your roguish ways?" Odette asked. "It wasn't so long ago that you abandoned your position as a Knight of the Golden Sun in favor of treasure hunting. Now it's like you have long forgotten that. I think you have been spending too much time around the palace walls. And Lumina." Odette said that last bit with a teasing smile.

Pryvyd blushed a slight red in the moonlight. "The only one that has been pushing me to be more noble again is Righteous."

The hovering arm gave a big thumbs-up and then patted the bald knight on the back.

"And he has done a pretty good job. Mostly because I can't seem to get rid of him."

Righteous changed his friendly pat into a slap across the back of Pryvyd's head.

"I'm kidding," the knight said, waving his left hand over his head to block another smack from Righteous.

Moshul turned back to the others and put a large mossy finger up to where his lips would be if he had them. Then he gestured to Roveeka, who was resting on his shoulders and fast asleep.

"How does she do that?" Odette asked. "She can sleep anywhere."

"Oh yeah," Wily added with a chuckle. "I've seen her sleep through a full-scale ambush, swords clashing all around her. It's been one of her secret skills since she was a toddler."

"Well," Pryvyd added, "let's not wake her. We could all use a little rest when we can get it tonight."

It wasn't more than an hour before Wily saw a large cloth tent surrounded by lit torches stuck into the ground. The tent was made of black-and-white fabric woven into a hypnotic swirl that seemed to vibrate in the flickering light of the burning wood stakes. Around the outside of the tent, mounts and carriages could be seen parked and waiting for those inside.

"Do you see a snagglecart?" Wily asked.

"Not yet," Pryvyd said as they approached. "But that doesn't mean it's not on the other side of the tent or hidden in the hills nearby."

As they got closer still, Wily could hear the cheers of rowdy patrons screaming from within. Pryvyd pulled up to an unoccupied post near a pack of riding snakes, which hissed menacingly at the horses. Moshul prodded Roveeka, stirring her awake.

"Just a few more hours," she said as she lifted her heavy lids. Once she saw what lay ahead, she immediately sprang to attention.

"Don't worry," Odette said to her mare. "The riding snakes are tied up."

"They look pretty slithery," Roveeka said. "What if they slip out of their harnesses?"

"Righteous will stand guard to make sure they don't hurt the horses," Odette said. "Is that okay with you, Righteous?"

The hovering arm saluted Odette proudly before pulling its sword from Pryvyd's sheath.

"Look what I see," Pryvyd said, gesturing to a spot near the back of the tent.

Wily looked where Pryvyd was pointing, and his heart dropped. A rush of nightmarish memories flooded him. He recalled seeing carts just like this one terrorize the peaceful residents of Vale Village while his father watched from the high wall of a rolling prisonaut. This was without a doubt a snagglecart. Then he remembered that the first time he had seen his mother, although he hadn't known it was her at the time, had been during the very same battle. How strange to think that his family had been reunited under such strange circumstances, with none of them aware of the significance of the moment until much later.

"If you see my father leave the tent," Wily said, "hold on to him. And don't let go."

Righteous gave an even prouder salute as if to say, "I will not disappoint you."

The inside of the tent was much larger than it

appeared on the outside. Wily wondered if the same magic that was used on everstuff satchels was being used here in the Dirty Vagabond. Food and drink stalls formed concentric circles around the large caged area at the center of the tent. Wily could see (and smell) how the traveling tent had gotten its name. No one in the whole place appeared to have showered or bathed in the last decade; even the pale-skinned moon elves were gray with dirt and grime. Looking around, Wily spied many types of creatures he had never seen before. Some were similar to humans and gwarves but had horns sprouting from odd parts of their bodies, like their shoulders and chins. Others were far more bizarre, like the completely translucent beings that resembled walking mounds of mucus, leaving trails of slime in their path.

As Wily and his companions moved toward a cabbage beer bar, he could see that many of the odd customers were giving them sideways glances. He wondered if they recognized them or if this was how all new guests at the Dirty Vagabond were treated. Or maybe they stood out simply because they were so clean compared to everybody else.

Pryvyd put his single fist on the counter and gave it a loud knock.

"Can I get a cabbage beer?" he said throwing a few coins down on the counter.

The bartender grabbed a grimy glass off a rack and stuck it under the nozzle of a wooden barrel. The glass filled with pale green liquid that fizzed like a pool of acid. As he slid it over to Pryvyd, Wily caught a whiff of the malodorous beverage and wondered if perhaps it wasn't just the customers who were stinking up the tent.

"Are you going to actually drink that?" Odette asked.

"It's an acquired taste," Pryvyd said, taking a sip. His face screwed into a grimace, and it looked like it took every ounce of control for him to refrain from spitting the liquid back into the glass. "Clearly one I haven't acquired yet."

A few stools down from Wily, a rowdy squatling smashed a glass over the head of a scar-faced hobgoblet.

"I'm going to punch your teeth out," the hobgoblet screamed at the top of his lungs.

"You're too late for that!" the squatling said with a big toothless growl.

The two began trading blows while other customers of the cabbage beer bar continued to go about their business as if nothing out of the ordinary was happening.

"Any sign of your dad?" Roveeka asked Wily quietly.

"Not yet," Wily answered.

"Let's see if we have better luck near the cage," Pryvyd said, leaving the barely touched cabbage beer on the counter.

The cage was a large dome of metal nearly as tall as the tent itself. Wires stretched across the middle of the dome, forming a horizontal web that hung a full story off the ground. A jousting match was in progress high up in the web. A pair of ghost spiders, both adorned with colored silks, were snapping at each other with their mandibles as the gwarves, strapped to their backs, swung wooden axes at each other. The gwarf wearing the green armor seemed to be doing a much better job than the gwarf in the bronze armor, clobbering his opponent's shoulder over and over.

"Knock him down, greenie!" a lanky troll called out between swigs.

"We want to see a fall," a pale moon elf yelled, his fingers wrapped around the metal mesh of the cage.

The emerald-armored gwarf slammed his opponent in the shin, causing him to begin to slip from his saddle.

"Hit him again, greenie!" the lanky troll shouted with glee.

But before the green-armored gwarf could strike, the bronze gwarf's spider gave a powerful bite to the opposing arachnid's foreleg. With a scream, both the green-plated gwarf and his spider went tumbling from the web above to the hard dirt ground of the cage.

A huge group of bystanders on the other side of the cage erupted in a chorus of cheers.

"That's a horrible game," Roveeka said. "Even Stalag wasn't that mean."

Wily disagreed with Roveeka on this point. He had witnessed Stalag, the former master of Carrion Tomb, incinerate rats with a flick of his wrist and imprison noble heroes in the mines to do his bidding without giving it a second thought. Spider jousting was a cruel sport for both the gwarves and the ghost spiders, but for that very reason, Stalag would probably enjoy watching it immensely.

"Next match will be a triple-header," a hobgoblet screamed from the side of the cage. "Three spiders! Three gwarves! One winner! Don't leave now unless you want to miss all the excitement."

Wily was disgusted. This was excitement he could live without. The only important thing right now was finding his father, and unless he was wearing a very elaborate disguise (which was possible), Kestrel Gromanov should be very easy to spot.

"Let's check the noodle stalls next," Pryvyd said. "All the strongest foot soldiers hang out there."

"You just want to eat something that will get the taste of cabbage beer off your tongue," Odette said.

"That's not the only reason," Pryvyd said, rubbing his tongue against the back of his hand. "Although it is one."

Wily was about to follow Pryvyd when a pair of spectacles caught his eye. On the other side of the cage, near where the batch of ghost spiders and gwarves were suiting up for the next match, a hooded figure was staring at him. Beneath the hood, Wily could see a pair of glasses resting on a nose. They looked just like the pair his father wore. Wily couldn't make out the face behind the glasses, though.

Wily shifted back and forth, trying to better his

line of sight. The figure was talking to a gwarf beside the door to the cage. Pryvyd, Moshul, and Odette had already moved in the direction of the noodle stalls. Only Roveeka had stayed behind with Wily.

"What is it?" Roveeka asked.

Wily turned to his half sister.

"I need you to use your hobgoblet vision," Wily said. "Is that man in the hood my father?"

Wily turned back to point at the hooded figure, who had moved into the light of a glowing torch. With the figure's face now illuminated, he didn't need his half sister's keen vision to tell him that his father was staring right at him.

"I found him!" Wily shouted to his companions.

Wily watched as Kestrel said something to the gwarf and shoved a pouch of gold into his hand. The gwarf responded by throwing open the gate of the cage. The three ghost spiders seized their opportunity and skittered out into the main portion of the tent.

Panic erupted almost immediately. The crowd that only moments ago had been cheering for blood was now fleeing in terror as the ghost spiders crawled along the outside of the cage, hungrily looking for food. A spider decorated with orange-and-yellow silks pounced on top of the slither troll that had been rooting for the green-armored gwarf and started gnawing on his arm. The troll tried to scratch his way to freedom, but was not doing a very good job of it.

Wily turned his focus back to his father, who was smiling calmly. Then he shrugged as if to say *nice try*.

Just then, a large glob of saliva dropped on Wily's shoulder. Looking up, he found himself staring at the clicking mandibles of a ghost spider.

"You look tasty," the spider clicked in Arachnid.

Wily was fluent in many languages, including the one spiders used to converse. It was a skill that was required of any talented trapsmith.

"Why eat me?" Wily clicked in response. "I'm not the one holding you captive."

"Have you ever eaten a gwarf?" the spider answered. "They're tough and bony and their beard hairs get caught in your teeth."

"Well, I suppose you do know better than me," Wily answered honestly.

The spider dropped from above, landing on Wily. The tips of its pointy legs dug into the soft flesh of Wily's exposed arms. He feared that he was about to have more scars join the long one that already stretched from his elbow to his wrist. Then he realized that what he should really worry about was that there would be no arm left to display a scar after the spider was done with him.

Wily pulled his screwdriver off his trapsmith belt and jabbed the spider in the soft part under his jaw. Wily knew that while it might hurt the spider for a moment, it would leave no permanent damage. He had used this trick before, during his many years in Carrion Tomb.

The hungry arachnid released its grip, giving Wily a chance to slide out from under it.

Moshul grabbed the spider by the abdomen and threw it across the tent. The eight-legged creature slammed into a stack of cabbage beer barrels, causing them to burst into a geyser of pungent green.

"Where was he?" Odette asked Wily urgently.

Wily pointed to the gate in the cage from which the spiders had been released. Of course, his father was nowhere to be seen. Even the gwarf that his father had paid was gone.

"He'll be going for the snagglecart," Pryvyd said. "Hopefully Righteous has already got its grip on him."

Odette took off into the crowd, leapfrogging over slither trolls and boarcus. Wily and the rest of the group struggled to keep up with her as they cut through the back of a shellfish stall, where elves were shucking oysters with sharp forks. Other patrons of the Dirty Vagabond were fleeing the chaos of the tent as well, and Wily found himself elbowing his way among throngs of filthy ruffians.

Pushing aside the black-and-white curtains, Wily found himself back out in the torch-lit carriage grounds surrounding the tent. At first he was disoriented, having emerged from a different door than the one through which he had entered. The hobgoblets and squatlings swarming past him, eager to get as far away from the ravaging spiders as possible, didn't help him get his bearings either. He was on the backside of the tent, farthest from the road. He turned to see Righteous guarding the unoccupied snagglecart. Wily knew that there were hundreds of mounts there. His father could steal any one of them.

"Over there," Roveeka said as she tugged on Wily's sleeve.

Roveeka was pointing to a group of horses near the side of the road. The hooded figure that Wily was certain was his father was mounting one. Wily took off at once, hurrying through the glowing torches, riding snakes, and horses to the road.

"Odette! Moshul!" Wily shouted. "Over here!"

Moving closer, Wily watched as a second figure mounted a horse next to his father's. A pair of bony hands stretched out from the sleeves of its cloak. The skin on each was so translucent you could see the blood pulsing through the veins beneath it. Wily knew at once who this was: Stalag.

The cavern mage pointed his fingertips toward Wily, firing off arrows of crackling darkness. Wily dropped to the dirt as the magical bolts zipped overhead. Roveeka dove to Wily's side as more of Stalag's bolts struck the ropes and chains holding a group of horses in place. Other arrows hit the animals' flanks, sending them into a wild panic.

Horses charged in every direction as Wily rolled out of the way of the pounding hooves. He looked over to see Roveeka burying her face in the dirt. A carriage pulled by two giant stallions was rolling right for her. She had no idea she was about to be trampled.

"Roveeka," Wily shouted. "You've got to move!"

With only a moment to spare, Odette performed a front handspring, grabbing Roveeka in her arms and tugging her out of danger. Wily quickly turned his attention back to Kestrel and Stalag, who were preparing to ride off.

"Don't let them get away," Wily shouted to Moshul, who was stepping over gwarves and horses that were running past.

Wily could see Stalag start to mutter as he pointed to one of the loose riding snakes slithering through the crowd. The cavern mage's magic spell struck its target. He watched as the snake began to rapidly grow. The horses that had been frightened by the magical bolts were doubly terrified by the snake that was now roughly the size of a full-grown crab dragon.

Moshul came to a stop as the giant reptile blocked his path to Wily's evil fathers. Pryvyd and Righteous tried to run around the snake, but the giant creature lifted its head and showed its fangs.

"Easy, big guy," Pryvyd said, trying to calm the snake. "We just want to get around you."

In response, the snake snapped at Pryvyd, leaving a pair of fang-shaped dents in his bronze armor.

"Maybe you should let Wily handle the beast quelling," Odette called out from nearby.

Wily could see that beyond the hissing beast, Stalag and Kestrel were galloping off. He jumped to his feet and approached the snake cautiously.

"I know you're frightened," Wily said in Gargle tongue, "but I promise the spell will wear off soon."

"I don't like this," the snake replied. "I feel a great hunger in my belly."

"That's going to pass as soon as you shrink down," Wily said in his most soothing tone. Stalag and Kestrel were getting farther away. "Just curl up and wait for your rider to return."

"So hungry," the snake said as he began to circle Wily. "I will eat you."

"Hold your breath," Odette shouted.

Before Wily had a chance to react, a yellow mushroom landed at his feet. It exploded into a plume of smoke. Wily inhaled the vapor and everything went dark.

WILY WAS JOSTLED awake. Odette had both her hands on his shoulders and was shaking him vigorously. He looked over to see that the giant snake was dozing nearby. Its tail and neck had been restrained in case it woke up before it shrank. Pryvyd and Righteous, who had collected their horses while Wily was asleep, stood nearby.

"Did they get away?" Wily asked his friends, who were watching over him.

"Yes," Roveeka said. "But you're not in a snake's belly, so that's good."

"They were heading off to the west," Pryvyd said. "And we think we know where they are going."

"Ratgull Harbor," Odette said.

"What makes you guess that?" Wily asked as he sat up.

"Look what we found in the snagglecart," Odette replied.

She handed him a small leather book. He opened it up. It was filled with his father's handwriting. Each page was either a journal entry, blueprint, or map. Odette flipped to the last page with writing on it. On the top it read: "The Riddle of Drakesmith Island."

"Drakesmith Island?" Wily said, recalling the name. "That's where the Eversteel Forge is rumored to be. I was gifted a crown made of unbreakable metal that came from the island."

"No one knows exactly where it is," Odette said. "Some say it's beyond the Salt Isles. Others guess it is far off in the South Ocean. It seems as if your father may have figured out the true location."

"I know for a fact he's wanted to find the Eversteel Forge for decades," Pryvyd added.

"Why would he leave the book behind?" Wily asked. "It doesn't make sense."

"He was in a rush," Roveeka said.

"No," Wily countered, "he is too careful for that.

He left it here on purpose. He wants us to know about Drakesmith Island."

"You're reading too much into our good fortune," Odette said. "It's the only clue we have. I think we should consider ourselves lucky we have a clue at all."

"If Stalag and Kestrel are off to find a hidden island," Pryvyd said, "they're going to need a ship. And every ocean-faring ship on the west coast of Panthasos is in Ratgull Harbor. Not that I am suggesting we continue on that path. I think we should head back for the palace. Get Lumina and Valor and then we can all make a decision together."

After a moment of consideration, Wily stood up and leaped onto the back of his horse.

"Perhaps if we move fast, we can catch them before they reach the harbor," he said with determination. Then he turned to Pryvyd. "I know you want what's best for me. But this is a risk we need to take."

Pryvyd sighed, realizing he wasn't going to be changing any minds this evening.

"Think of the adventure ahead," Odette said with a grin.

"Right now, I'm only thinking about the danger."

Wily was thinking of something else. He looked to the western horizon, where he could imagine the two figures riding off side by side. He felt anger bubbling up inside him. His two horrible fathers were working together again.

4

THE RATS OF
RATGULL HARBOR

The dawn swallows left their nests just before the sun peeked over the horizon. Flitting from the twisted branches of the tawny pines, they took to the sky, letting the light of the soon-to-be-rising sun paint their white feathers a soft pink. It was a beautiful sight, but Wily could barely lift his head to see it.

The group of adventurers had been riding for three days since they had left the Dirty Vagabond, with very little rest. An occasional stop to let the horses drink and eat had been the only times Wily had spent out of the saddle. Roveeka had caught some deep sleep when Moshul agreed to carry her in his arms like a baby being cradled by her father.

"I should have purchased a bowl of noodles back at the Dirty Vagabond," Odette said as she ran her fingers through her long blue hair. "I'm crazy hungry."

"You can fill your belly at Ratgull Harbor," Wily said, feeling his own stomach grumble too. "We can't risk letting my father and Stalag get too far ahead of us."

Nearly every moment of the last three days, Wily had been thinking of his two mortal enemies in league with each other. His birth father, Kestrel, had imprisoned him in Carrion Tomb with the evil cavern mage Stalag for the first dozen or so years of his life, while he wreaked terror across the kingdom. Then after Kestrel was imprisoned it was Stalag's turn for a reign of terror. He had been solely responsible for building the army of stone golems that nearly destroyed the land. Wily could only imagine what the two would do now that their forces were combined.

"What's so important about Drakesmith Island and the Eversteel Forge anyway?" Roveeka asked the group from Moshul's shoulders.

"Swords and axes made in the belly of the forge can cut through stone as if it were made of candle wax," Pryvyd said. "Armor pulled from the forge is tougher than ten-foot-thick steel walls."

"And a machine built from parts made in the forge would be impossible to destroy," Wily added. "Impish and Gremlin would never be able to bust one apart. Moshul's fists wouldn't be able to crush it. Think of the new gear-folk, snagglecarts, and prisonauts my father would be able to build. It would mean the return of the Infernal King, and this time he would be truly invincible."

"Then why didn't your father try to find it before?" Roveeka asked.

"He did," Pryvyd replied. "When I was still under the command of the king, before I realized what a horrible tyrant he was, a group of Knights of the Golden Sun was sent out to find it. They were the bravest warriors and sailors in all the land. They never came back. We sent a second group of men and women after that. They never returned either. By then Kestrel was already controlling Panthasos with an iron fist. We had no need to send out another party to try to find the Eversteel Forge."

"He must have learned something in the prisonaut," Odette said. "New clues he had never heard before."

"But how?" Roveeka asked.

"There were many cavern mages trapped in there with him," Odette said. "Who knows what they could have learned from their dark magic?"

"Or what Stalag might have discovered while he was in hiding," Pryvyd added. "Perhaps he brought the new information."

Roveeka nodded, then seemed to brighten as she looked ahead.

"I think I see the city we are heading for," she called out. "At least I think it is a city."

When the horses reached the next rise, Wily understood why Roveeka was slightly doubtful. Through the gentle mist, the port town itself looked as if a great wave had washed hundreds of ships out of the harbor and onto the shore. The overturned boats jutted up at strange angles, exposing their barnacle-covered bellies to the sky. Metal anchors dangled from the bows of the boats like candle-less chandeliers. A spiral of stacked rowboats looked like a giant staircase reaching toward the clouds. What at first seemed like a chaotic mess was anything but. Wily realized the boats had not been haphazardly tossed but instead carefully placed along twisting roads and footpaths. The painted hulls of ships were rooftops, with portholes serving as windows and doors to the strange buildings. Chunks of broken pier had been used to create a wall that bordered the city.

"Long ago, Ratgull Harbor had only a single bait shop," Pryvyd said, "a few houses, and a dock. When the locals wished to expand, rather than gathering fresh wood from the nearest forest, which was a full day's ride away, they took a shortcut and just used the planks and boards from an abandoned ship that had washed onto the rocky beach. Not long after, when the town was ready to grow again, a particularly lazy builder realized he could cut even more corners by dragging a whole ship right onto the shore, flipping over, and turning it into a building. From that point on, it just became cheaper to buy old ships and turn them into houses rather than build houses from scratch."

"I think it is quite pretty," Roveeka said.

"Agreed," Odette said. "Shall we go and get a closer look?"

The group followed a broken shell trail down to the entrance of town. A large sail attached to a mast stuck into the ground swung with the breeze. Written in black squid ink across the white fabric were the words RAT-GULL HARBOR WELCOMES ALL. In slightly smaller lettering below, the words THE LAWS OF PANTHASOS DO NOT APPLY BEYOND THIS POINT were also written.

"What does that mean?" Wily asked, eyeing the slightly off-putting statement.

"It just means they have their own way of doing things here," Pryvyd said. "There is no mayor or ruler of this port. Just businessfolk out to make a profit."

"I'll fit right in," Odette said with a smile.

As they passed underneath the entrance sail, an easterly breeze swept across the harbor, filling Wily's nose with the smell of rotting oysters and squid guts. If he had been hungry before, he certainly wasn't now. The group dismounted their steeds and tied them to nearby horse posts. Then they moved down a narrow avenue between two schooners, each of which had been tipped so the fronts of the great sailing vessels pointed to the west. The one to the right had a wooden bust of a woman with flowing ringlets carved into the bow and the words LADY SEAFOAM painted beneath. A dozen seagulls sat on her head, cawing loudly. A pair of elves with strands of seaweed in their hair stood by the strange building's front door.

"Driftwood for sale," the elderly elf said as she

plucked long hairs from her ears. "Gathered it off the beach this morning. Still salty and wet for bending."

"Not today," Roveeka said as they passed.

"Have you seen a pair of hooded men on horseback passing through here?" Wily asked.

"Is one as pale as a fist of bone coral?" the elf asked. "And the other wears spectacles of bronze?"

"Indeed. That sounds like them."

"Then, yes," the elf said. "Just this morning. They were heading down to the schooner docks. Odd pair. Didn't look like the seafaring type."

"The schooner docks?" Wily said. "Which way is that?"

"Just cut down this alley back here."

THE GROUP TOOK the elf's directions down a tight, winding road. The buildings on either side creaked as the wind blew through the loose boards holding them together. They hadn't made it far when a group of skrovers, overgrown rodents that rather disconcertingly had learned to walk on only their hind legs and enjoyed a reputation for being rather unpleasant and untrustworthy, surrounded the group.

"Hand over all the coin in your pockets," the nastiest of the skrovers said as he hoisted a pointy wooden stick. "And your weapons too."

"Is that an old soup spoon?" Odette asked, eyeing the piece of wood in the skrover's front paw. "Are you trying to rob us with a spoon?"

"Well, yes," the skrover said. Then he fingered the pointy end. "But I sharpened it real good and now it could poke out an eye."

"I've seen him do it," one of the other skrovers said.

"And it don't feel good," said another skrover with a patch over his eye.

"I would actually like to keep both my eyes," Roveeka whispered to the others.

"Now give us your coin," the leader of the skrovers said.

Suddenly, the sewer grate below them popped open and a dozen brine elves and gwarves sprang out, each holding throwing sea stars.

"This is a mugging," the salt-encrusted gwarf said. "Hand over ye valuables."

"Sorry," Pryvyd said. "You're a bit too late. We're already being mugged by someone else."

"It's true," the skrover said, turning his sharpened spoon on the gwarves and elves. "We got to them first."

"I saw them right when they came under the entrance sail," the gwarf said, clearly frustrated.

"Then you should have robbed them there and then," the skrover said. "They be ours now."

"I needed to round up a gang," the gwarf complained. "I couldn't have taken them alone."

"That's not my problem," the skrover snapped.

The gwarf looked around at the group of barely armed skrovers.

"This is all you brought?" the gwarf asked. "They have a golem on their side. How did you think you were going to defeat them? With that old spoon?"

"I sharpened it real good," the skrover said a little defensively. "It can take out an eye."

The skrover with the eye patch nodded. "And it don't feel good."

Wily looked at the gwarf. And kept staring at him. The gwarf looked very familiar.

"Have we met before?" Wily said.

"Maybe," the gwarf said. "Are you the kid who sells crab claws down in the muck tunnels?"

"Nope," Wily said. Then it clicked into place. "In the Floating City. I met you there. You're friends with Needlepocket, the bounty hunter. I remember now. Your name is Scullygump."

The gwarf was taken aback. And maybe a little flattered.

"That's right, I am," he said. "You remembered my name!"

"What brought you to Ratgull Harbor?" Roveeka asked, treating the mugger as a new friend.

"After the new prince took over," Scullygump said, "the Floating City wasn't the best place for burglemeistering. Too many guards keeping order and making things safe. Here in Ratgull, the same rules do not apply."

"We're heading for the schooner docks," Pryvyd said. "If you take us there, we can make it worth your while."

"Well, then what are we waiting for?" Scullygump turned back to the other gwarves and brine elves. "The mugging is called off. Go back to your scavenging."

The elves and gwarves, disappointed, turned and headed for the entrance to the sewer tunnels.

"Right this way," Scullygump said as he pointed the companions in the direction of the harbor.

As the group started to head off down the road, the skrover started waving his wooden spoon in the air.

"Aren't you forgetting something?" he said. "We're robbing you of all your money."

"Maybe another day," Roveeka called back brightly.

Scullygump led them through the maze of dry-docked boats to a long pier where dozens of sailing vessels were being relieved of their cargo. They moved past dockhands loading a sailing vessel with crates marked with the words EXTREMELY DANGEROUS—DO NOT OPEN WITHOUT GLOVES. Wily could only wonder what lay within the wooden walls of the bolted boxes.

"THIS IS THE place you were looking for," Scullygump said with an outstretched hand. Pryvyd slipped a few coins into the gwarf's palm. Before Scullygump had even pocketed them, he had scampered off, grunting with delight.

Odette moved to a stack of barrels and bounded to the top of the pyramid. She cupped her hands on either side of her mouth and shouted to the sailors on the pier in her loudest voice.

"We are looking for a pair of men that might have been seeking passage to Drakesmith Island? We will pay for information."

A great murmur followed, and dozens of sailors began shouting over one another. Each was eager for some quick change.

One voice spoke louder than the rest. "If you are willing to pay, you might as well spend it on something more than information."

Wily looked up to see a tall man in a black silk vest, satin pantaloons, and a scarf as colorful as the ones his mother had worn. He was leaning over the railing of a magnificent ship that looked particularly out of place among the less impressive ships surrounding it. It was built from wood as gray as an overcast sky. The figure-head decorating the front of the boat was carved in the shape of fox, its bushy tail melding with the front railing of the vessel. A crew of brine elves were busy scrubbing down the decks with soapy brushes. Others were loading up crates from the dock into the hold of the ship.

"They sailed out of the harbor this morning on the

Squall Singer," the curious individual said, to the groans of the other greedy sailors who would have been able to pass on the same information for a few gold coins.

"We need to catch that ship," Odette said to the crowd. The majority of the sailors sighed and went back to their work.

"The ship is extremely fast," the same sailor continued. "And with the wind offshore blowing in from the south, the vessel will be making doubly good time. None of these vessels have a chance of catching up with the *Squall Singer.*"

The satin-pantalooned sailor swung down to the pier on a dangling halyard line. Wily could now see that on his bare feet, each toe was painted with either purple or dark blue nail polish.

"Except one. My ship. The *Coal Fox* charter ship. I'm Captain Thrush Flannigan."

Odette eyed him skeptically. "And how would the *Coal Fox* do what the others can't?"

"By taking a shortcut through the Drecks. A stretch of windless sea that the *Squall Singer* will have to circumnavigate. Even a schooner with the tallest sails finds itself drifting aimlessly there."

"I don't understand," Roveeka said, scratching the side of her bumpy head.

"The *Coal Fox* is an experimental vessel with sails and enchanted oars. It can move even without the wind. And I would be willing to take you for a price."

"How much would that be?" Pryvyd asked, already seeming not so keen on the answer.

"I've heard the stories told of you, Pryvyd Rucka," Thrush said. "And you too, Wily Snare, Prince of Panthasos. I am quite sure you will pay more than I need."

Wily looked to Odette for her thoughts. She was already smiling as she stared at the sailing ship.

"They left a few hours ago," Thrush said. "There really is no time to waste."

"Then we leave at once," Wily said, eyeing the gray ship.

Thrush gave Wily a bow. "Welcome aboard, Your Majesty." Then he turned back to the brine elves on the ship. He shouted to them, "We have new, more important cargo to transport. Dump the cargo. Prepare the guide gulls. We leave at once."

With that, Thrush grabbed the dangling line he'd swung down on and hoisted himself back up onto the deck. He approached a long wooden board and, with a kick of his boot, knocked it over the side of the *Coal Fox*. One end came crashing down right at Pryvyd's feet. It formed a ramp from the dock up to the ship's deck.

"All aboard," Thrush said. "Let's catch the *Squall Singer*."

5

THE *COAL FOX*

As the crew of the *Coal Fox* skittered about the deck like pincer crabs, Wily looked back at the docks and dense clusters of buildings that made up the bustling harbor town. From a distance, Ratgull Harbor appeared to be far more majestic and far less decrepit than it actually was. The charter ship, with a single sail raised, slowly drifted toward the mouth of the bay in the light wind.

"It's time for the oars!" Thrush called to his crew.

As they passed the last of the large ships and houseboats moored in the bay, Wily heard the sound of metal grinding against metal. It was a sound he knew well: gears. He followed the noise to an open hatch in the deck. He peered inside to see that the belly of the *Coal Fox* was an enormous machine. The rows of oars that jutted out from either side of the boat were not magical but mechanical. Gears activated pistons, which pushed the oars back and forth in a steady rhythmic pattern.

"Incredible, isn't it?" Thrush said, coming up behind Wily.

"Did you build it yourself?" Wily asked, fascinated by this incredible machine.

"I can sail it better than anyone in Panthasos or beyond," Thrush continued. "But I, even with the most detailed schematics, could never have built this beast. This was constructed by a brilliant inventor, the most brilliant one ever to live. You might recognize the name. I believe your father named you after him: Wily Snare."

It was true. Wily had been named after the famous inventor who had written his father's favorite book, *Wily Snare's Book of Inventions*. Never once had Wily seen one of his namesake's inventions turned from an idea into an actuality, though.

"I didn't know any of his inventions still existed," Wily said in awe.

"We've worked hard to keep this one in good working condition. The brine elves change the gears and levers once a month to keep them from corroding. And we make sure never to pass too close to the Salt Isles, where the air is so corrosive it rusts metal within hours. In fact, it's the only place this ship is forced to steer clear of."

Wily watched as the winches and pistons turned the oar handles in perfect synchronization. Ever since he'd found a copy of the book of inventions in Squalor Keep, Wily had been fascinated by the illustrations within it (even if he had trouble reading all the words), but to see one of these machines in action was a special treat.

"Approaching the open sea," a brine elf shouted from the bow of the ship.

Wily moved to the side railing and took in the view. Two jetties of stone formed the narrow exit of the harbor, only wide enough for a pair of ships to pass safely through at one time. As they slipped out of the mouth of the bay, Wily looked at the vast ocean ahead. It left him in a state of complete awe. It was a similar feeling to when he had first experienced the Above and looked up at the sky, stunned by its impossible vastness and beauty. More surprising than the magnitude was how the sea seemed to be in a constant state of motion. Wily understood how water rushed in a stream, in one direction from the highest point to the lowest, but he couldn't figure out what was making these rolling waves of water surge across the level ocean. As the *Coal Fox* pulled farther away from shore, he watched as the sunlight caught the tips of each rolling wave for a moment before each dipped into the dark blue again. The crew shut off the oars as the wind took over, the sail pushing them swiftly ahead.

After many minutes of gazing, Wily's attention turned to Thrush and one of the brine elf crewmembers, who were talking quietly by the wheel of the ship. The brine elf held a closed wooden box with a small door on its side.

"Send them out," Thrush said with a glance to the open sea.

The brine elf opened the door slightly and began whispering inside. When he was finished talking, he opened the box's door wide. A trio of gray gulls flew out and took to the sky. Two of them circled the ship before beating their wings and soaring off to the west. The third gull flew to the top of the tallest mast and took a seat on the high perch that Wily had heard referred to as the crow's nest.

Thrush, seeing Wily's curiosity, explained that these were guide gulls, trained to find things in the vastness of the ocean and report back to the ship once they had accomplished their mission. They would be able to locate the ship Wily's father was on and then return to give direction on how best to pursue the *Squall Singer*.

As Thrush was just finishing explaining, Pryvyd hurried past the two of them to the railing. His face was a pale shade of green and his lips were chapped and dry. He had pulled off his gauntlet and was wiping his face with his palm. Odette came up alongside him and gave him a pat on the back.

"Are you feeling seasick?" Odette snickered. "The same Knight of the Golden Sun who was dreaming of fleeing Panthasos for the Salt Isles? Come now, I know you've been on boats before."

"Never one that tossed and bobbed like this one," Pryvyd said as he gulped a lungful of air.

Righteous floated up to Pryvyd's side and hovered near. It was clear the floating arm was enjoying this too.

"Oh, don't give me that," Pryvyd said to Righteous. "If you were still attached to me, your knuckles would be just as pale as mine."

Righteous just waved a finger as if to say, *Not true.*

Wily saw Roveeka sitting at the bow of the ship, her legs dangling through the holes in the railing. As he walked closer, he could see she was using one of her knives, Pops, to carve a piece of driftwood.

"What are you making?" Wily asked as he sat down next to her.

"I was trying to make a birk," Roveeka said. (She was still confused by the word *bird* and always seemed to get it wrong.) "But I cut off the head."

"I'm sure we can find you another piece of wood," Wily said as the salty spray splashed against his bare ankles.

"Nah," Roveeka replied as she took long strokes with her knife. "I feel like this knotty piece of driftwood deserves a second chance. I'm not ready to toss it into the sea quite yet."

Roveeka tilted her head up to glance at the guide gull still sitting in the crow's nest at the top of the mast. She attempted to carve the bird's head again to the very best of her ability, which right now seemed to be a bit lacking. Wily turned to the ocean before him and stared into the distance. There was nothing to see besides clusters of gray clouds and the occasional fish fin sticking out of the icy waters. His mind wandered, thinking about how he would confront Kestrel Gromanov when he finally caught up with him. Moshul would grab him tight and shake him until he couldn't take it any longer. He would make his father wish he had never left the prisonaut.

When he snapped out of his long daydream, he realized his mind was not the only thing drifting: the boat was too. They had come to a portion of the ocean that was completely calm; not even the gentlest breeze fluttered through their sails.

"We've reached the Drecks," a brine elf called out from the side deck.

"This is why the *Coal Fox* is the most valuable ship on the seas," Thrush said from behind the wheel. Then he shouted to the crew members: "Bring down the sail. And crank up the oars again."

A mohawked elf hurried over to a large bronze lever near the mast. With a strong pull, the lever made a grinding sound. Wily peered over the railing to see the oars jut out from the side of the ship. With each synchronized pull, they sent the *Coal Fox* racing forward.

"Stay this course," Thrush said as he stared out at the clouds ahead.

The charter ship plowed into the heart of the Drecks,

passing mounds of dead fish that bobbed on the surface of the water, filling the air with a foul odor.

"Debris from the entire ocean drifts here and swirls around endlessly," Thrush said as he pointed to a mass of floating wooden cups and chicken bones. "You can see that the ocean has become a dumping ground for what land folk don't want. And it all ends up here. Keeps growing and growing every year. Even a small ship can find itself stuck here with no way to escape. Look out there. A whole island of seaweed."

Wily could see a mass of pale green vegetation drift by in the distance. Although he couldn't be sure, it seemed like there might even be animals scurrying on top of it. Wily felt a heavy tap on his shoulder. Moshul was now standing beside him and pointing to a patch of water much closer, where half of a boat drifted past, its hull cracked and splintered.

Moshul signed something to Pryvyd, who was no longer looking quite as green as before. The calm ocean seemed to have calmed his stomach.

"I'm not sure what caused it," Pryvyd replied.

"It must have hit a reef," Thrush said, spotting the broken ship. "Without a set of oars, whirlpools can be quite dangerous here. We'll be able to steer right around them, though. Nothing to worry about for us."

Moshul pointed to another mass of wood. It appeared to be the other half of the boat.

Just then, something flew out of the water. A sea

bass, roughly the size of a cow, soared through the air and landed on the deck with a horrifying thud.

"Did that fish just jump out of the water?" Roveeka asked as she dropped the piece of driftwood she was still attempting to carve.

"I don't think it jumped," Odette said. "I think it was thrown."

"What makes you say that?" Roveeka inquired.

"It's missing a head."

Wily looked down at the sea bass and found a most disturbing sight. The fish's eyes, mouth, and neck were all gone, cleanly bitten off by what had to be a giant set of teeth.

"Are you sure that boat hit rocks?" Wily called out to Thrush with rising fear in his voice. "Because the rocks I know don't have giant teeth."

"Or leave sucker marks," Odette added, pointing to the side of the giant fish.

Moshul suddenly looked terrified. He hated anything with tentacles, no matter how big or small. And clearly whatever had killed this sea bass was awfully large. Thrush peered over at the fish and his whole attitude changed.

"That's bad," Thrush said. "Those are the marks of a salvage squid. On rare occasion, they come to the Drecks to feast on an easy target."

Moshul signed something quickly.

Odette responded with words and signs. "Well, I don't want to be an easy meal either."

"Turn the ship around!" Thrush screamed to his crew. "Use oars and sails. Use everything!"

The crew scrambled across the deck in a panic, pulling lines and raising the sail. Another brine elf started pressing buttons on the panel near the oar lever. Thrush turned the wheel as he peered out into the still waters.

"Over there," a brine elf screamed, pointing behind the ship. "I saw something move beneath the surface."

"By Glothmurk!" Thrush muttered to himself. "This isn't what I signed up for."

"If we turn back," Wily said with alarm, "my father will get away."

"If we don't turn back," Thrush replied, "we'll be at the bottom of the ocean with the sea ogres."

The *Coal Fox* was about halfway through its turn when a giant tentacle burst from the water, slid onto the deck, and wrapped itself around the leg of a brine elf.

"Get it off me," the brine elf cried as she was lifted high into the air.

No one on board had a chance to do anything before the rubbery arm plunged back into the sea with the elf still gripped tightly in it.

"Can you talk with it?" Odette asked Wily.

"Squid are not much for reason," Wily answered.

"Even the nice ones have only two-track minds: grab and eat."

"Keep turning the boat around," Thrush commanded his crew.

"Shouldn't we be getting out our swords and bows?" Pryvyd called to Thrush as he pulled his shield and Righteous drew its blade from Pryvyd's holster.

"And what good do you think an arrow would do to a salvage squid?" Thrush said. "Not even your golem throwing a punch would do the trick. And right now, your golem doesn't look like he is going to do much more than hide in the corner."

Wily looked over to see that Moshul was curled up at the center of the deck, cowering. Roveeka was standing beside him, patting him gently.

"It's okay to be scared," Roveeka said. "Everyone gets scared sometimes. I know I do all the time. Most of the time actually. Just stay next to me."

"Actually," Odette said as another tentacle came sweeping across the deck, "we could really use his help right now!"

There were now five of the creature's eight arms out of the water. Two were wrapping suckers around the bow of the boat while the other three were swiping crew members off their feet and into the sea.

"It's too late!" Thrush shouted.

Wily was desperately trying to come up with an idea for what they could do. He wished the oars had

66

turned the boat around a little faster. They would have been free and on their way. He looked at the sails and the lines. *Is there a way to build ourselves out of trouble? There's no time to construct a whole new machine, not with the squid attacking us.* Then the beginning of an idea came to him: *Maybe I don't need to build a whole new machine, but just modify the one that has already been built.*

"Odette! Roveeka! Moshul!" Wily shouted. "Come with me."

Wily ran to the hatch leading belowdecks and flipped it open. He bounded down the steps into the hold. The maze of gears, pulleys, and levers reminded him of the maintenance tunnels inside Carrion Tomb, where he had spent many quiet hours greasing the gears of the crushing walls and refilling the poison in the darts of the blowgun tunnel. Wily grabbed a pair of wrenches off his toolbelt and handed one to Roveeka and the other to Odette.

"Start unscrewing the lug nuts on the back of each of these handles," Wily said as he pointed to the oars attached to the rowing machine. "Like this." He pulled out his screwdriver and with twelve quick turns of his wrist popped four screws free. An oar fell to the wooden floor with a clatter.

"Detach the oars?" Odette asked with alarm. "How is that going to make this boat go faster?"

"We're not going to be using the oars to row." Wily

picked up the oar and handed it to Moshul. "Snap the paddle off."

Moshul took the long piece of wood in his hands and cracked the wider end of the oar off, leaving only a pointy splintered end.

"Just like that," Wily said with a big grin. "Do that to all of them."

As the words came out of his mouth, the ship made an unpleasant creaking sound, as if the hull was being strained by the force of the squid's mighty arms.

"As fast as you can," Wily added urgently.

Wily set off on his own task. He detached the piston that had moved one oar back and forth and repositioned it so he could stick the oar handle directly inside it.

"If we are not making this ship row faster, what are we doing?" Odette asked as she continued to unscrew the bolts with the wrench.

"This automated rowing machine is using all the same mechanics as one of the traps I had to maintain in Carrion Tomb: the blowgun tunnel."

"That's great to hear," Odette answered. "But still not understanding."

"Instead of using the oars to row," Wily said as he hammered, "we're going to make the pistons fire the oars out like darts. Very big darts."

Wily picked up the oar Moshul had snapped and shoved the smooth tip into the open piston and pointed the splintered tip toward the porthole. Wily reached into one of his pouches and pulled out a small vial of pale cobra venom. It was the same poison he had used in the trip-wire tunnel back in the tomb. He placed three drops on the very tip of the splintered oar.

Above, Wily could hear the screams of the brine elves. Below, the wooden hull was creaking louder. Water was beginning to leak through the seams on the sides of the ship. There was no time to waste.

Odette, Roveeka, and Moshul helped Wily as he raced around inside the cabin. They converted five of the seven other oars into sharpened spears, lacing each one with the poison. Before they could start on the sixth, a tentacle slid in through the porthole near Wily, squirming and searching for something to grab. Wily jumped back but not fast enough: the tentacle wrapped around his leg, the suckers vacuuming tight to his clothes and skin. Wily knew from experience with the cave squid in his youth that once an octopod tightens its grip, there is little chance of breaking free. Wily grabbed tight to the gears of the rowing machine as the aquatic beast gave a sharp tug. His fingers were not going to be able to hold on much longer.

WHAP. Moshul's giant green hand came smashing down on the salvage squid's tentacle. It must have greatly startled the creature because it released its grip long enough for Wily to slip free and drag himself to cover.

"Thanks," Wily signed to Moshul. "I know that must have really frightened you."

Moshul signed back as Odette translated.

"Terrified. But I was even more scared you were going to be hurt."

The four companions put the last oars into place. With the machine ready, Wily and the others ran back for the stairs to the main deck. When they reached the top, Wily found that things were much worse than he had feared. The mast had been snapped from the ship, and the salvage squid was swinging it like a club, causing the entire crew to duck as it swept it low over the deck.

"What were you doing down there?" Thrush screamed. "The ship is barely moving at all now. There's no way we can escape at this speed."

Wily ran to the wheel as he shouted. "We need to lure the squid to the surface. Get its body out of the water and around the ship."

"Are you crazy?" Thrush yelled. "That's exactly what we have been trying to avoid!"

"Trust me. It's our only chance."

Thrush glanced at Wily with a look of utter disbelief. Then he spun around and shouted in his loudest voice.

"Everyone stop fighting the squid. Let it take the ship!"

The brine elves looked horrified. They dropped their swords to their sides and backed toward the center of the vessel. Only Righteous continued to fight.

"You heard the captain, Righteous," Pryvyd shouted. "Stop fighting."

If Righteous heard its former body's command, it didn't pay him any heed. Wily ran up to the hovering arm's side.

"Please," Wily said. "Back off."

Righteous reluctantly lowered its weapon. It floated away from the enormous rubbery arm it was doing battle with.

Wily hurried over to the lever that activated the machine below. The squid's tentacles slithered farther across the deck, the suckers making loud squishing sounds as the squid latched onto the gray wooden planks.

"Do it now!" Odette shouted.

"Not yet," Wily said with bated breath. "We only get one shot with this."

The *Coal Fox* was trembling like a small animal being choked to death. Then, bursting from the deep, came a triangular head with two eyes as large as dining room tables. The salvage squid had a black beak that snapped, mumbling in Gurglespeak as it did.

"Grab!" the salvage squid said. "Grab! Grab!"

Its tentacles wrapped tighter around the ship as its body rose out of the water.

"Wily, now!" Odette insisted again.

Just then, a tentacle slid over the edge of the railing and grabbed Roveeka around the leg.

"Eat! Eat! Eat!"

Wily grabbed the lever of the repurposed machine and pulled. The sound of gears twisting into place was followed by a loud series of booms as the pistons shot out the oars. Seven oars went soaring over the surface of the ocean, missing their mark. The eighth, however, made a splurging sound as it went through the rubbery skin of the salvage squid.

The tentacle with Roveeka held tight for a moment, then relaxed its grip, sending her dropping toward the ocean. Righteous flew across and grabbed the hobgoblet, keeping her from falling into the water. Moshul grabbed Roveeka and Righteous and pulled them back onto the boat as the squid let out a gurgling scream.

The squid flailed as it attempted to pull the sharp oar from its side.

"Grab! Grab! Graaaa . . ."

Its tentacles went limp as the venom of the pale cobra took effect. With a mighty splash that soaked the entire crew, the salvage squid plunged into the sea and drifted down toward the bottom of the ocean.

The crew of brine elves began to cheer as Wily hurried back toward the hatch.

"Where are you going?" Odette asked.

"I'm not sure how long the venom's effect will last on a creature as big as the salvage squid. I need to turn the machine back into a rowing machine so we are far away by the time it wakes up."

Wily swung open the hatch but stopped before going downstairs.

"We're also going to need to find something to use

for oars," Wily said. "Like those wooden railings. They'll work."

Wily dipped below the deck with a smile on his face. He had avoided disaster. Their search for his father could continue.

6

ISLAND BEYOND THE FOG

Wily's lips felt as if he had eaten an entire plate of salted mushroom caps. Even the insides of his cheeks lacked moisture. Moments ago, he had drunk an entire jug of water and still he felt thirsty. After a full night of rowing through the Drecks, the *Coal Fox* had finally left the breezeless portion of sea behind and passed into a dense fog that Thrush had said must have picked up the salty air that hangs over the Salt Isles. The guide gulls kept reporting back to the ship with news that they were making progress catching up with the *Squall Singer*, but as of yet, Wily had not caught a glimpse of the elusive ship.

"Echh," Odette said from her seat next to Wily on the wooden deck. "Even I can't be cheerful on a morning like this. How can anyone stand this?"

"My lips taste like over-seasoned slugs," Roveeka said. "I like it."

"Figures," Odette replied. She stood up and walked over to Moshul, who was sitting at the very front of the ship, letting the wind blow through the blades of grass growing between the clumps of moss on his shoulders.

"You mind if a pluck an aqua leek?" Odette asked.

Moshul shook his head and gestured to his knee. Odette pulled a long shoot from the golem's knee, then held it over her mouth and gave it a squeeze. A small waterfall poured out from one end, giving Odette a long drink. She walked back to Wily and handed it to him.

"We're getting closer to the Salt Isles," Thrush said. "We'll steer clear soon. The air does more than parch throats. Stings the eyes until they are nothing more than balls of pink. And it rusts metal within hours."

"And you wanted to live there?" Roveeka asked Odette and Pryvyd.

"It would have kept us away from the Infernal King," Pryvyd said. "That's worth some irritated eyes."

"To think that now we are out here chasing after him," Odette said.

Just then the outline of an island came into focus through the thinning fog. It was short and flat and covered in yellow reeds that swayed in the gentle breeze. The forest of trees beyond the reeds was different from any vegetation Wily had seen in Panthasos. The trees had spiky needles sticking out from them in addition to giant pale green leaves. They reminded him of cave urchins on a skewer. The sun pushed through the clouds, dappling the waves with light. Suddenly, the island's beach sparkled like a million shards of broken glass had been sprinkled along the edge of the sea.

"Not many people set foot on the Salt Isles," Thrush said. "They are used more as way points than destinations. They're far too dangerous to set foot on. Savage beasts, part animal, part mineral, live on them. And that's only a fraction of the problem. Even the toughest metal rusts away. Which makes getting back off particularly tough. This ship won't get closer than Oris Rock."

Thrush pointed off the starboard bow as he took a sip of his bubbly water. Wily could see a rock that jutted up from the ocean like a falcon's head. Flags of many colors were strung around the rock like necklaces. Wooden objects like bows and salad bowls dangled on ropes from it, knocking together like a strange wind chime in the breeze.

"What's all that stuff on the rock?" Roveeka asked.

"Oris was the great falcon knight of yesteryear," Thrush said. "He was the one responsible for returning Glothmurk to the bottom of Skull Trench. Oris is said to still watch over the sea. Keep people safe from the things that lurk in the deep. Sailors say it's good luck to leave something here for the bird spirit in exchange for good fortune going forward."

"I'm guessing you haven't given an offering lately," Pryvyd said. "On account of the salvage squid."

"Or did I?" Thrush said. "We got out alive. That's a stroke of good luck."

"It was Wily's smart thinking," Odette said, "not the Falcon Knight that got us out of trouble."

"But perhaps it was the Falcon Knight who brought him to me." Thrush looked at Wily. "I didn't get a chance to thank you yesterday for all you did to save the *Coal Fox*."

"The truth is you wouldn't have been in any trouble at all if I hadn't come to borrow your ship," Wily said. "So I'm the one in your debt."

"You're a good kid," Thrush said with an odd tone in his voice. "The kingdom would be in good hands if you were the one in charge."

"Thanks," Wily said. "That means a lot to me. To be honest, I sometimes doubt it myself."

"You shouldn't," Thrush said. "And I just needed you to hear my appreciation before I did this." Suddenly his entire demeanor changed. He turned to his crew and shouted: "Now!"

Within moments, Wily and his companions were surrounded by every brine elf on deck, all pointing swords and knives at them. Thrush himself grabbed Roveeka and held her tightly, pressing a dagger to her throat while still clutching his glass of bubbly water in his other hand.

"What are you doing?" Wily cried.

"Leaving something behind on Oris Rock for good luck," Thrush said with a sympathetic frown. "This is where you all get off."

The brine elves pushed a wooden plank out over the ocean.

"If you jump off nicely," Thrush continued, "nobody has to get hurt. Perhaps you'll even be able to make it to the island over there, assuming you're good swimmers, of course." Thrush led Roveeka toward the plank.

"This is high treason," Pryvyd said as he pulled his shield off his back. "You'll spend the rest of your life in a prisonaut for this."

"I made a trade to save Ratgull Harbor," Thrush said. "I was told to bring you here. To get you far away from Panthasos. And dump you in the ocean. If I didn't, the cavern mage said he would wipe all Ratgull Harbor off the map when they took power. I am sacrificing you to save the city and people I love."

"I knew there was something shady about you," Odette said.

"Am I a villain or a hero?" Thrush said. "Ask the people of Ratgull Harbor in five years."

"A murderer is never a hero!" Wily spat back.

"I only promised to dump you in the ocean beyond the salt fog. I'm not going to kill you."

"How generous," Odette said.

"Quite," Thrush said. "Considering the alternative. I am truly sorry how this all happened. I genuinely think you would make a good king. But rulers come and go. Ratgull Harbor must persist." Thrush took a swallow of bubbly water as he moved the dagger closer to Roveeka's throat. "Who's swimming first?"

"I'll go." Pryvyd didn't hesitate. "Just don't hurt Roveeka." He walked straight off the plank and plunged into the water. Righteous flew out over the water, hovering just a few feet above its former body.

"You promise to let her go?" Wily asked, looking at the fear in his sister's eyes.

"Do you really think that I want to be stuck with a hobgoblet on my vessel? I just need to give you a little encouragement to get off the *Coal Fox*. Then she'll be joining you."

Wily ran down the plank and jumped. He was in the air for only a second before he plunged into the cold ocean water, the impact nearly knocking his trapsmith belt right off his body. Still underwater, Wily opened his eyes. Even with the bright sunlight streaming in from above, he could see only forty feet below; beyond that everything went black. It was like he was floating over a bottomless hole. And it was nearly silent. Below the surface everything was still and quiet. For a moment it reminded him of the long hours he spent lying in his bed with the door shut back in Carrion Tomb, all the sounds of the dungeon muted by the thick rock walls of his room. The flash of memory was interrupted by the sharp pang of his lungs tightening as they drained of air. Just then, the water exploded with bubbles as Moshul cannonballed into the sea.

Wily kicked back up to the surface. As his head emerged from the water, the screams of the brine elves and the loud slaps of the waves hitting the side of the *Coal Fox* came rushing to his ears.

"Grab on to me," Pryvyd said from the water nearby.

"No way," Wily said. "You've got to try to stay afloat with that armor. You don't need me weighing you down."

"Remember the halo wax," Pryvyd said. "This armor is practically a floatation device."

Wily had forgotten that the Knights of the Golden Sun coated the inside of their armor with a magical wax that was lighter than air. It made carrying a suit of armor less of a burden for the long hours they spent patrolling and protecting the kingdom. On their last adventure, Wily and his friends had coated the rocks at the Lava Crown with halo wax to make them float over the fiery volcano.

Wily grabbed hold of Pryvyd's shoulder as Odette jumped into the water as well, performing a perfect dive and surfacing just an arm's length away. She seemed to make any feat of physical activity look ridiculously easy, no matter how difficult it actually was.

Thrush came to the side of the *Coal Fox* with

Roveeka still held at dagger point. "I wish you much luck," Thrush said as he tossed Roveeka into the ocean. "You're going to need it."

Wily watched helplessly as the *Coal Fox* used its mechanical oars to turn back in the direction of Panthasos.

"Is everyone okay?" Odette asked as waves bobbed her up and down.

"Besides being terrified?" Roveeka asked. "That took a lot out of me. I'm not brave like the rest of you."

"We need to swim for the island," Pryvyd said.

Wily looked across at the Salt Isles. The distance didn't seem so far, but he knew that this was deceptive. And who knew what was lurking in the water beneath!

"And fast," Odette added as she pointed to a bank of storm clouds coming closer, arcs of lightning dancing between them. Pryvyd took off his armor.

"If we all hold on to one side of the armor," Pryvyd said, "and let Moshul do most of the kicking, we should be able to keep our strength and make it across."

Once everyone was in position around the floating armor, Moshul began kicking. The golem's powerful legs pushed them along steadily. Wily had practiced swimming in the underground pools of Carrion Tomb and was quite adept, but this was completely different. With every wave, water splashed into his mouth and eyes, leaving him spitting every couple of seconds. As they moved slowly toward the island, Wily thought he felt blobs of jelly rubbing up against his ankles. Yet each time he stuck his head below water to see what was the cause of the strange sensation, nothing was there. Wily wondered if the sea was filled with invisible fish or if they were just too quick to spot.

It seemed like Moshul had been kicking for hours, but they appeared to be no closer to the Salt Isles at all. The hot noon sun was pelting down on the group. Wily thought it was strange to feel chilled and blisteringly hot at the same time, but the long swim was accomplishing both.

As Moshul continued to kick, Wily spied something large and blue moving beneath them. It took only a moment to realize the creature below was actually not a single creature but an entire school of blue-eyed opals. The fish circled around the group and began to nibble bugs and shoots off Moshul's legs.

Moshul signed with one hand.

"I'm sure it's not pleasant," Pryvyd said. "But at least sharks aren't nibbling on us. Your plants will grow back."

As Moshul's legs grew tired, Wily and the others had to start kicking along with him. After just a few minutes, Wily was reminded of what it had felt like rolling the boulder back into place in Carrion Tomb, time after time. Endless. He looked out at the island and wondered if they had made any progress at all.

Then, to everyone's surprise, Moshul was suddenly towering over them. He was standing on solid ground.

They had reached the shallows. Yet they were still a great distance from shore. Moshul, despite seeming exhausted, signaled for everyone to climb up on his shoulders. With tired arms, Wily pulled himself up and sat in the perch that was usually Roveeka's spot.

"Huh," Wily said to his sister. "It really is nice up here."

"I told you," the hobgoblet said with a smile.

Moshul took huge slow steps through the water. Wily could peer down and see the rocky ground below. Colorful sea stars and crustaceans dotted the sandy bottom. As they got ever closer to the island and the water became shallower and shallower, Wily was able to fully appreciate the size of the Salt Isles. The one they were approaching was not the tiny speck in the sea he had first thought. It stretched for what seemed like miles in both directions.

"It's even saltier here than it is out in the ocean," Wily said, puckering his lips. As the waves hit the rocks, plumes of spray churned the air with white flakes that were carried by the wind like snow blowing from a high peak. After another hundred steps, Moshul was putting the group down on the shore. Wily could now see that what appeared to be glass from a distance was actually very fine salt crystals catching the sunlight and reflecting it back in every direction. It was so bright he had to shield his eyes. The reeds hugging the side of the beach were tough and yellow, with thick roots that dove deep into the earth.

Wily lay back on the beach of salt and let his body sink into the fine granules. Despite knowing nothing about this island, he was overjoyed to be on it right now. If he had his wish, he wouldn't swim again for years.

As Wily stared at the sky, he could hear a soft rustling by his ear. He looked over to see a pair of thumbnail-size yellow crabs lifting their eye stalks for a better view of Wily's curly brown hair. They seemed to like what they saw because they began to try to find their way into his locks.

"You don't want to hide in there," Wily said with a smile. "I bet there is a rock or a seashell that would make a better home."

Wily reached out a finger but the crabs backed away cautiously.

"I won't hurt you," Wily clicked.

Suddenly, a loud shriek pierced the air. The spooky sound came from the jungle. It was quickly echoed by a second and a third shriek, identical to the first. Then, more and more screams. It was almost as if the entire jungle had come alive.

Wily sat up with alarm, as did all of his companions. Everyone peered into the reeds looking for the animals making the noises.

"It sounds like the whole jungle is screaming," Roveeka said.

"It is," Odette said ominously.

She pointed to one of the strange trees with needles

sticking out from its bark. It had a large knot in its trunk that was moving. Or at least it first appeared to be a knot. It took Wily a moment to realize what he was seeing. The tree had a mouth—and it was screaming!

7

THE SCREAMING TREES

"Do you think the trees were people placed under some horrible curse?" Pryvyd asked the others as he cautiously walked up the beach toward a row of the screaming palms. "Doomed to cry out in pain for centuries?"

"Why don't you ask them?" Odette said. "They have mouths. Maybe they can answer."

"Can you speak?" Pryvyd said as he approached one of the trees. In response, it only screamed louder than before. Pryvyd backed away. "I'll take that as a 'no.'"

Moshul began to sign to the others. "I don't think it was a curse," Odette translated. "They must have evolved this way to scare animals away from them. Plants can be very smart like that."

"I think that the needles sticking out from them

would be reason enough not to bother them," Roveeka said.

Moshul signed again. "Fresh water must be very valuable on this island. The plants don't want that to be stolen from them. Animals like the one that made those." Moshul pointed to a spot at the top of the beach where white hoof marks were visible in the salt.

Roveeka approached the prints curiously and leaned down. She jabbed her finger into the print and then scooped up a handful of white flakes.

"What type of mineral is that?" Pryvyd asked the hobgoblet.

If Roveeka had one area of expertise it would be . . . knife throwing, but coming in a very close second would be her knowledge of all things geological. Whether a rock, stone, or gem, Wily's sister could identify it and tell you a hundred facts about it.

Roveeka held the flakes to her nose, then stuck out her tongue and licked them.

"Eww," Odette said. "Why would you do that?"

"They're halite crystals," Roveeka said with a grin. "We grind them up in the dungeon to get salt."

"The animal must have stepped in salt and brought it here on its hooves," Pryvyd said.

"Or," Roveeka proposed, "the animal could be completely made of salt and it just leaves a path of halite crystals wherever it goes."

"I think my version is a lot more likely," Pryvyd said.

"I disagree," Roveeka said. "On account of . . . behind you."

Wily and Pryvyd both turned around at the same time. Before them stood a pig as big as a wolf, with a white crystal face and a set of translucent tusks. Its thick stone legs were kicking the sand angrily, sending flakes of salt into a cloud behind it. The strange creature looked like it was preparing to charge.

Righteous was the first to act. It flew forward with sword in hand. The salt boar swung its tusks to parry the blade—and as soon as contact was made, Righteous's sword turned to rust and crumbled. The boar lunged forward and snapped down on the armor plating surrounding Righteous's hand. Then it began to mash the bronze armor in his teeth and chew it like a cracker.

"That's my arm you got in your mouth, pig," Pryvyd said, grabbing Righteous by the hand and tugging it free. Angry at the interruption of a promising meal, the salt boar turned its attention toward the knight, eyeing his shiny breastplate as its mouth watered. "Oh, no you don't."

Pryvyd grabbed his armor and tossed it away before the boar could nosh on it. This enraged the crystal beast, which let out a bellow. The trees echoed the boar's scream, with the sound seeming to travel miles down the beach and deep into the jungle. Then the salt boar charged at Pryvyd, brandishing its crystal tusks. Pryvyd blocked the attack with his spiked shield, but just as the sword had, the shield shattered upon impact with the strange creature. The boar let out another cry as it kicked up more salt.

"Get away," Odette screamed as the boar jabbed its tusks toward Pryvyd.

The Knight of the Golden Sun tumbled backward and was nearly impaled, but Moshul grabbed the boar in his moss-covered hands, lifting it off the ground. The boar flailed, trying to pierce the golem, but it only managed to shave vines from his chest. Once Moshul got a good grip, he spun the boar in circles overhead before tossing the crystal creature into the ocean. The salt boar sank below the surface, disappearing into the waves.

"Do you think it will come back?" Roveeka asked as she stared out at the ocean.

"Unfortunately," Wily said. "I don't think a little water is going to keep it away for very long."

"Worse still," Odette said, "I fear more may be on the way."

"Do you think you could quell them?" Roveeka asked Wily. "You're amazing with monsters."

"That creature seems more rock than animal," Wily said. "I think my beast-training skills won't be helpful."

Righteous, who was hovering nearby, looked very alarmed. The armor that had once encased the arm became brittle and fell to the ground like metallic snow, revealing Righteous's true form beneath. Wily realized he had never seen the transparent ghostly appendage without its protective shell before. Despite loving Righteous dearly, Wily found its new appearance a little creepy. The arm looked sad and defeated.

"The salt from the boar sped up the rusting," Pryvyd said, looking over at Righteous. "But it would have happened with or without the boar."

"It's true," Wily said. "Even the buckles on my trap-smith belt are beginning to crumble."

"Oris Rock is looking pretty good right now," Pryvyd said. "With or without a storm. It would be better than here."

"I'm never swimming again," Wily said. "Or at least not today."

"Then what do you propose we do?" Odette asked.

"We make camp and use some carefully constructed traps to keep the boars out," Wily said. "It's building time."

"But everything made of metal is falling apart," Odette said. "What kind of traps can you possibly make without metal?"

"We can make drop pits with wooden spikes and cover them with leaves," Wily said. "It won't be fancy, but it can keep us safe."

"Drop pits with spikes?" Roveeka asked. "I don't want to hurt the pigs . . . even if they are kind of mean."

"If we point the spikes downward along the inside walls of the trap," Wily explained, "no animal will get hurt. Including us. But it will keep them contained for a while."

Wily's mind switched into trapsmith mode. His eyes darted around the beach, composing a plan.

"We can't make camp here," Wily said. "We need to find a spot in the jungle where the ground is more solid."

Everyone except for Wily eyed the line of screaming trees with caution. He knew there was little time.

"We need to act now," Wily said. "Before a whole herd of salt boars shows up."

Together, the group hurried off the sand and through the chorus of moaning palms. Wily was looking for something very specific: an unoccupied patch of earth a good ten feet away from trees in every direction. After a few minutes of running, Wily found a spot that would have to do.

"Here," Wily pointed to the center of the ring of trees. "Put all our stuff in the center. Moshul, I need you to dig a trench in the dirt that looks just like this." Wily used a stick to form a large circle around the center spot, then a second, smaller circle inside it. "It needs to be this wide, and as deep as Pryvyd is tall." Moshul nodded and set to work digging, his large moss fingers pushing into the thick, heavy earth. The moss golem's fingers dug off the top layer of soil and salt. Right beneath, Wily saw a dense network of roots.

Moshul signed as Odette translated. "This will make digging a little tougher. The trees have adapted to the island. Their roots go deep into the ground to find fresh water. I will have to pull them out too."

"Do what you have to," Wily shouted, raising his voice over the sound of the screaming trees. "I need the rest of you to collect reeds, leaves, and branches. We have to cover the trench as best we can."

Wily and Roveeka split off in one direction, scanning the ground for palm leaves. They were surprisingly hard to find. It seemed as if these trees held on to their pale green leaves more than a typical bush or plant did.

"I haven't found any but this one," Roveeka said, holding up a shriveled brown leaf in her hand. "I guess we could try pulling them off." As she uttered the words, a nearby palm began to wail loudly. "Sorry. I didn't mean that."

"Look, I found a whole bunch of sticks under here." Wily pointed to a large fallen limb. "And some leaves too."

"Hopefully," Roveeka said, "Pryvyd and Odette found more than we did."

Wily and Roveeka ran back toward the camp with their meager find. When they got back, they discovered that Moshul, despite the dense mesh of roots, was a much faster digger than they were leaf finders. Three quarters of the trench was already complete, and judging by the speed with which Moshul was working, Wily was certain it wouldn't take him too much longer.

"We've got plenty of leaves," Pryvyd said as he came back with an armload. Odette was close behind.

"It wasn't pleasant," Odette said. "We had to do a bit of delicate climbing and plucking to get all these. You think hearing those trees scream on the beach was bad. Try cutting leaves off their branches. I can barely hear myself think. Plus, I have some pretty nasty scrapes from those needles."

Moshul finished digging out the trench, which was now a full ring around the plot of earth in the middle. Wily and the others snapped branches, making them into wooden spikes that Moshul then lined the inside wall of the trench with. Once finished, the moss golem climbed out.

"Cover the drop pit with leaves and twigs," Wily instructed the others. Once they were finished, it was impossible to see any evidence of the trap hidden below (with the exception of the large amount of leaves in one area). Moshul and Pryvyd placed a log across the gap to allow the group to move to the center island. Once they were safely together in the small circle of earth, Pryvyd and Moshul pulled the log over to their side.

It was close quarters in their makeshift camp. The group was practically shoulder to shoulder. Wily wished he had suggested making the circle in the center of the trap larger. It wouldn't have taken that much more effort on Moshul's part, and it would have been a whole lot roomier.

"I think we should have made this little island a little less little," Odette said as she tried to stretch out her legs without hitting anybody else.

"Really? I like it," Roveeka said. "It feels like we're a family this way. Hobgoblets sleep in big piles on the ground."

"I'm wet and tired and I really don't want anybody's elbow in my face," Odette said as she nudged Righteous, who was hovering just over her head. "Float a little higher, will you?"

The long day had taken a toll on the perky morning elf. Then again, the long day had taken a toll on Wily too. He had thought he was so clever, getting Thrush to take them on the *Coal Fox*, and now here they were, stranded on a deserted island, without a chance of catching up to his father and Stalag.

I made another mistake. How could I be so foolish? He felt like crying, but his eyes were so dry he couldn't even squeeze out a single tear.

Wily wiggled about, trying to make himself comfortable, with little success.

"We're going to be okay," Roveeka said quietly in his ear. "Right?"

Wily turned and gave a weak smile back. As he did, he could feel his body trembling. At first, he was confused. He wasn't cold or even nervous. Why was he shaking? He quickly realized that Roveeka was shaking too. In fact, everything was vibrating. Then he heard the noise: a low rumbling like that of a crab dragon trying to dig its way through a stone wall.

"I think the salt boars are coming," Pryvyd said as the rumbling grew louder.

The sound of storming feet was joined by the wailing of screaming palms. It was only moments later when the stampede of salt boars, with tusks pointy and snouts huffing, came blasting out of the jungle. They were heading straight for Wily and his friends. Wily had a moment of sudden panic that these animals might be capable of jumping farther than he'd anticipated. If that was the case, they would all be poked like pincushions.

Luckily, the trap he had devised functioned exactly as intended: the lead boar's halite hooves made contact with the fake floor of leaves and twigs, and the branches snapped and gave way to the pit beneath. The surprised animal dropped inside. The boars behind it were moving too fast to stop before reaching the edge of the trap. Like a waterfall of fur and crystal, the mass of boars went tumbling, one after the next, into the hole.

Wily looked down at the snorting, angry mass of wild animals thrashing below them. The few boars that had managed to slow themselves before falling into the pit paced anxiously around the circle looking for some way to reach Wily and his companions. Some of the boars in the pit tried to climb over the others to reach the adventurers, but the spikes that had been placed around the center prevented it. Soon the boars grew frustrated and realized they had been bested. They scrambled back up the outside wall of the trench, scurried past the still-wailing trees, and disappeared into the jungle.

"We did it," Roveeka said with a big smile.

"But now what?" Odette asked. "We spend the rest of our lives trapped here?"

"When dawn arrives," Pryvyd said, "we'll start building a raft. We're going to get off this island and stop Kestrel. I promise you that. But for now, in the dark, all we can do is rest."

"Which is hard to do," Wily said, "knowing that my father has not only escaped the prisonaut but is now with Stalag searching for the Eversteel Forge."

Righteous was squeezing its fist in anger, ready to take on Kestrel and Stalag all on its own.

"I'm angry too," Pryvyd said.

Roveeka nestled up next to Moshul and then turned to her brother. "There's room for you here too, Wily." Wily crawled beside her and got himself comfortable, resting his head on Moshul's cool, mossy body. The soft vegetation reminded Wily of his pillow back in the royal palace, his home that seemed so very far away right now.

WILY WOKE UP alone. His friends were nowhere to be seen. The log had been laid down across the trench that Moshul had dug. He could feel his throat was dry again like part of a sandy beach where the waves never reach.

"Odette? Pryvyd?" Wily called out. He walked across the log to the other side, carefully making sure that there were no boars hiding among the trees. "Roveeka?"

Wily saw footprints on the ground that led in the direction of the beach. He followed them as he tried to wet his lips, which felt like potato crisps. The morning sun was creeping over the horizon, casting the clouds in a pink-and-orange light. The water lapped calmly against the shore as a salty mist drifted through the reeds.

Not far from him, through the fog, Wily saw Righteous hovering beside Pryvyd, whose back was to him. He was dressed in his golden armor, as polished and shiny as it always was. But as Wily got closer, he could sense that there was something not quite right about him.

"Pryvyd," Wily called out, "where is everyone else?"

The figure turned around—but it was not Pryvyd. Inside the armor was Stalag, Wily's arch nemesis, his pale frame encased within the gold and metal. The evil cavern mage's eyes quivered with menace.

"They are all gone, you foolish boy," Stalag cackled. "Your mistake has led everyone to their doom. You will remain on this island until you are an old man, frail and weak and alone."

"No!" Wily screamed. "I'm not giving up. I will find a way off here."

"There is no second chance for you this time," Stalag said.

As he was speaking, the cavern mage's skin started to peel away from his flesh, and as Stalag smiled, hundreds of spiders began crawling out from the cracks in his golden armor. The hairy arachnids raced across the beach toward Wily, whose feet were now buried ankle-deep in the salt. Wily struggled, but before he could break free, the spiders were crawling all over him. He looked down to see one large black widow poke its sharp fangs into his arm.

As it bit down, Wily was snapped awake from his dream by his arm actually being poked.

It was dawn and all his friends were still gathered on the little island in the center of the trench Moshul had dug. Odette was next to him, her finger lightly jabbing his elbow.

"You were having a bad dream," she said.

"It felt so real," Wily replied.

"That's not the only reason I woke you, though," she added as she pointed above the trees. "Look."

Wily followed her line of sight out into the distance. A plume of white smoke was rising into the air.

"That's smoke from a campfire," Odette said. "We're not the only people on this island."

8

WHERE THERE'S SMOKE

"We should leave right now," Pryvyd said, staring out at the trail of white rising through the palms in the distance, "before whoever has lit the fire moves to a different spot."

"What if the salt boars attack us during our travels?" Odette translated for Moshul.

"It's a risk we will have to take."

Moshul laid down the log across the trench and the group departed their small island of safety for whatever dangers were lurking in the woods. To Wily's relief the screaming trees did not stretch deep into the jungle. Once they passed the last one, the jungle became quiet. At least, quiet for a short stretch. Soon Odette began whistling to herself.

"That's your happy whistle," Wily said to Odette. "Do you know something that we don't?"

"Huh," Odette replied. "I didn't even realize that I was whistling. Guess I'm just glad to be away from the salt boars."

Wily had his doubts about that. He wondered what pleasant thoughts were actually going through her mind. He watched her do a cartwheel into a handspring.

"Can you still see the smoke in the distance?" Odette asked Roveeka, who from her seat on Moshul had the best view through the trees.

"Yes," Roveeka said. "We are heading straight for it."

CLANK. Wily turned to see a large portion of Pryvyd's armor lying on the ground in broken pieces.

"Not much of my armor left now," Pryvyd said, trying to hold the remaining chest plate against his body. It snapped in half and crumbled to the ground, exposing the white cotton undershirt beneath. "What kind of knight will I be without armor?"

"The same as you are with," Roveeka said. "A great one. Except I'd stay out of battles. Especially ones where the other side has swords or arrows."

"My necklace crumbled to dust a while ago," Odette said. "Everything made of metal is disintegrating. Which is pretty fascinating."

Looking down at his tool belt, Wily could see that all his metallic tools had rusted over. He pulled out a flea wrench, used to turn the smallest bolts, and tapped the tip with his pinky. At once the wrench's metal prongs disintegrated, crumbling into red dust that drifted to the ground as a cloud of powder.

Wily turned to Roveeka, who was standing at his side in a sad slouch. Wily knew this was unusual for his hobgoblet sister.

"What's wrong?" Wily asked.

"It's Mum and Pops," she said glumly. "I can't bear to look."

Wily knew how important the two knives were to Roveeka, and so it was quite understandable that she was upset by the thought that they were nothing more than rust powder in her pocket sheaths.

"Then don't look," Wily said. "I know what they meant to you in the past. But they're just slivers of metal."

Roveeka smiled. "You're right." She gave the handles of the two knives on her waist a gentle touch with her forefingers.

"There's the campfire," Odette whispered from just ahead.

Beyond the last row of palm trees on the white salt beach, a fire of dried fronds and branches was burning. The steady plume of white smoke they had seen from a distance snaked into the sky before the wind blew it out to sea. Beside the fire, a small structure had been built of sticks.

"Can you see anybody?" Wily asked the others.

Not from up here, Moshul signed back.

"Maybe they are taking a swim," Roveeka said. "That would explain the shoes down by the water."

"Let's hurry over and investigate before they come back," Odette said.

As the group moved through the brush, Wily heard a distinct snapping sound nearby. From the leaf-covered ground, a rope net lifted into the air. Moshul was enveloped and hoisted off the ground. The hidden trap pulled the moss golem into the tree, which bent under his giant weight. Despite Moshul's great size, he was held aloft in the net.

"A trap," Odette said as she stepped backward. "There could be more—"

Suddenly Wily heard another snapping sound. Odette looked under her foot to realize she had just stepped on a trip wire.

"Whoops," she said.

A second net was pulled up from the ground. This one was just as large as the first that had snared Moshul, and it caught not only Odette but Pryvyd, Roveeka, and Wily too. Together they were lifted into the trees, their bodies tossed in the mesh of vine.

"That was my fault," Odette said timidly. "What? I'm allowed to make mistakes too."

"Righteous," Wily called out. "Where are you?"

"I think it's under my butt," Roveeka said.

"Nope," Odette answered. "That's my arm."

"It's down there," Pryvyd said.

Righteous, thin enough to slip through the holes in the net, had avoided capture and was hovering near the ground.

"Go," Pryvyd said. "Find where the rope is clamped and release us."

Wily watched as Righteous zipped up to the pulley hidden in the tree and then followed the path of the rope down to the ground. At the bottom, Righteous found that the rope was triple-knotted around a thick palm tree root.

"Untie it!" Odette shouted.

Righteous tried to pull the loops free, but untying a complicated knot with just one hand was proving rather difficult. It was a tight knot to start, and with the weight of all the heroes pulling it taut again every time Righteous managed to loosen it a little, the task seemed as if it might be impossible. Righteous gestured helplessly.

"Someone made this trap," Odette said, turning to Wily. "How would *they* get us down?"

Wily considered. "A simple snare like this one would be cut with a sword or knife or some other sharp blade."

"That's a problem," Odette replied. "Ours have all rusted away in the salt air. What do we do now?"

"We figure out some other way to cut the vines," Pryvyd said. "Perhaps we can find a sharp leaf that will do the job."

"A sharp leaf?" Odette questioned aloud. "You got one of those, Moshul?"

Moshul, hanging from the tree like a giant dewdrop of mud, shook his head as best as he could in the awkward position.

"Or I could just use my teeth," Odette said in a huff.

"That was going to be my next suggestion," Pryvyd said, sounding defeated.

"Mum! Pops!"

Wily twisted his neck, straining to look at Roveeka, who was pressed up against his back. She held in her warty hands her two knives. They were out of their sheaths, and to Roveeka's and Wily's surprise, they had not rusted at all. They appeared just as shiny as they had before they arrived on this island.

"How is that possible?" Odette asked, glancing at them.

"I guess they really are special," Roveeka said. "Mum and Pops have never let me down."

"It doesn't make any sense," Pryvyd said. "My armor and shield were far thicker."

"We can try to figure it out once we're down," Wily said. "Roveeka, cut through the ropes."

"I'm already on it," Roveeka said, hacking away at the vines beneath her. "Prepare yourselves for a pretty big—"

The net tore open. Pryvyd, Roveeka, Odette, and Wily fell to the ground.

"Ouch," Pryvyd said. "A little bit more warning would be nice next time."

"Didn't think Pops would still be so sharp," Roveeka said, "but he was. Never should have doubted him."

"No metal can survive the salt," Pryvyd said as he got to his feet.

"Unless Mum and Pops are eversteel," Roveeka said brightly. "Even when I don't polish them, they're always shiny."

Wily had often noticed the picture delicately drawn on the blades, which depicted what appeared to be a large sleeping lizard. When he was in Carrion Tomb, he thought the other markings along the blade were glowing torches. Since then, he had realized they were made to resemble the stars in the sky. *Was it possible that these blades were made in the mythic Eversteel Forge?*

Up above, Moshul was signing something to the effect of *I'm still up here and I don't want to be.*

Roveeka moved to the spot where the moss golem's snare was tied to a tree stump. With a quick slash of her knife, the rope was cut and Moshul fell to the ground with a thud. When the moss golem got to his feet, Wily could see that Moshul's head was dented and big chunks of mushrooms were smashed on top.

"From here on," Wily called to the others, "make every step a careful one."

Everyone nodded in agreement.

Wily approached the simple campsite, scanning the jungle floor for trip wires and drop pits. If there was one trap protecting the area, there were bound to be others as well. A few feet closer to the campfire, Wily found a patch of leaves laid out on the ground. With his foot, he carefully pushed them aside to reveal a pit with spikes made in an almost identical fashion to the trap they had made. There was just one major difference. The spikes in the pit pointed up, making the trap deadly rather than merely protective.

"Walk around the leaves," Wily called back to the others as he moved closer to the fire and the small wooden structure.

Odette walked up alongside him and peered into the flames.

"The fire won't last much longer without more wood," she said. "We should collect some before it goes out. It is far easier to keep a campfire burning than start a new one."

"Moshul," Pryvyd said, "stay here. Guard Wily. We'll be back with wood."

Righteous, Pryvyd, Odette, and Roveeka moved for the jungle. Cautiously, Wily peeked through the open door of the structure. There was nobody inside, just a collection of leaves that had been laid out on the floor like a carpet. Wily stepped underneath the roof of twigs and he found a few more items placed in a neat pile: a map scrawled on parchment, a pair of lenses that looked like they might have been from reading glasses, and the wooden handle of a tool. Wily was particularly interested in the map. He studied it closely, his fingers moving along the carefully drawn lines.

It appeared as if a small portion of the island had been explored and recreated on the sheet in black ink. Wily couldn't be certain, but he guessed it depicted places he and his companions had yet to pass. There was a drawing of a large plant near a stone temple, and along the shoreline a spot labeled "Grizzler Teeth."

By the time Wily stepped out of the small structure, Pryvyd and Odette were approaching the still-crackling fire, each with an armload of firewood. Moshul was scanning the area, both by using his jeweled eyes and by sending out a line of ants from his belly button to go exploring the nearby bushes.

"Hey, everyone," Wily said. "I found something that might be very helpful." But before Wily could tell the others what he had discovered, Odette interrupted him.

"Where's Roveeka?" Odette asked.

Moshul shrugged.

"I thought she was with you," Pryvyd said.

"She was," Odette said. "But she was tired so I told her to head back."

"On her own?" Pryvyd was mad.

"She's the only one with weapons," Odette said defensively. "I thought she would be fine. It wasn't that far."

"Roveeka!" Wily shouted with growing alarm.

From the shrubs, Wily heard a muffled voice cry out. Righteous leaped to attention. Even in the most spectral form, the enchanted arm was ready for a fight.

"Stay where you are," a man's voice shouted, "and the hobgoblet won't get a spear to the back."

Wily raised his hands in the air, as did the others.

"Let her go," Pryvyd shouted back. "We're not here to hurt anyone."

Roveeka took a few hesitant steps out of the bush. A sharpened bamboo pole was pressed to the base of her spine by a figure still cloaked in the shadows of the trees.

"Wily, I'm okay," Roveeka shouted, her voice trembling with fear.

"Well, well," the man's voice said. "This is getting ever more interesting."

Exiting from the foliage was a slight, middle-aged man with torn clothes and no shoes. Wily thought his eyes were playing a trick on him: the man was his father, Kestrel Gromanov, the Infernal King.

9

THE LOST KING

"I don't understand," Wily said. "What are you doing here?"

"Same as you," Kestrel said. "I'm stranded. I was made to walk the plank."

"By who?" Odette asked. "Your own crew?"

"It wasn't my crew," Kestrel said. "Stalag did this to me. He's responsible for all this. I didn't blow up the prisonaut. It was one of his spells."

"I found springs and gears all over the ground," Wily said. "There was no spell residue. You're lying, like you always do."

Wily's head was spinning. Why was his father here? What possible reason did Stalag and he have for making it seem like he was left here too?

"You have every reason not to trust me, son, but Stalag framed me," Kestrel said. "I had nothing to do with it. He was waiting for me outside the prisonaut with a snagglecart. He told me he discovered the coordinates of Drakesmith Island, home of the Eversteel Forge. He said we should travel there. That I could live a peaceful life far away from Panthasos if I helped him build a new army of gearfolk."

"You still escaped from prison," Wily said. "You didn't have to leave. You could have stayed in your cottage."

"That's true," Kestrel said, pressing the spear harder into Roveeka's back, "but I'm also not a fool. You would have kept me locked up forever."

"Then why are you here?" Pryvyd asked.

"Because Stalag lied," Kestrel said. "When we first left, he had me draw up plans for a new ubergearfolk. But it was all a ruse. He was distracting me from his true purpose. After we sailed around the Drecks, he and his men forced me to walk the plank. I barely managed to swim to shore."

"I don't understand," Wily said. "Why'd he stage the breakout only to dump you here? What was the point?"

"You followed me, didn't you?" Kestrel said. "Stalag knew you would. He left clues for you. He *wanted* you to come after me so he could dump you right here on the Salt Isles too. He wanted to get rid of everyone who could pose a threat to his plan to conquer all of Panthasos. He never hoped to find the Eversteel Forge. He doesn't even think it exists. He was just tempting me with something he knew I was interested in. He's been secretly rebuilding the old gearfolk with his magic. I saw one in person on the ship. It's wields a blade of dark energy. That's all he needs to take over Panthasos."

"He left the journal in the snagglecart on purpose," Odette said. "He wanted us to find it. To come after you. I'm such a fool for having fallen for it."

"You and me both," Kestrel said. "I thought he had just carelessly left it behind. He is far more clever than that. He was staging the whole situation. The old cavern mage has always been jealous of me. My life in the palace. My rule over Panthasos. I never realized just how much he wanted it all. Just how far he would go to get it."

"He seems to have pulled everything off perfectly," Pryvyd said morosely.

"We are trapped on the Salt Isles," Odette added, and for once her cheerfulness seemed to have deserted her. "Where no metal tools work and no machines can be built. We're stuck here, with no means of warning anybody in Panthasos of what Stalag has in store for them."

"All is not lost. Stalag underestimates my"—Kestrel eyed Wily closely—"*our* ingenuity. Machines can be made of wood and leaves and sand and stone. I am getting off this island and teaching that translucent old wizard a lesson."

"Did I hear you say 'our' ingenuity?" Odette asked. "I hope you don't think for even a fraction of a second that we are going to help you. Because I would rather eat a mouthful of sand— No. A whole beach of sand before I helped you."

"We want the same thing, elf," Kestrel said. "For Stalag to fail. We don't have to be fond of one another . . . just assist one another."

"Like we're going to trust you?" Pryvyd said. "You cut off my arm, remember?"

Righteous clenched its fist.

"Let bygones be gone," Kestrel said with a hint of a smile. "The past is in the past. Besides, your arm and you seem to be doing quite well apart. Perhaps I did you a favor."

"I'll do you a favor and remove your head from your neck, see how you like that," Pryvyd said, and Righteous gave his suggestion a big thumbs-up.

"You're a hero now," Kestrel said. "Heroes don't do such things."

"They do things like that to dragons and beasts," Pryvyd growled.

"I'm not a beast," Kestrel said. "And my time in the prisonaut has made me reconsider many of my choices."

"You're full of lies," Wily snapped. "You just said you promised to build Stalag a new army of ubergearfolk."

"I was never going to actually build him an army," Kestrel said. "I just told him I would. I figured once I got to Drakesmith I would disappear in the night."

Wily tried to read his father's expression.

"Aren't we all allowed second chances?" Kestrel said. "I am a different man."

To prove his point, Kestrel dropped the spear from Roveeka's back, allowing her to run to Wily's side. The two embraced as Kestrel stood with his pointed stick, watching.

"There," Kestrel said. "See? Different."

Wily was glad his father had freed Roveeka, but that didn't mean he was going to start trusting him all of a sudden.

"Different from four months ago when you stole my screwdriver so you could use it to escape?" Wily asked with an angry sneer.

"I admit it was a mistake," Kestrel said. "But I ended up returning that screwdriver to the warden."

"Whatever story you tell is not good enough for me," Odette said. "You were responsible for my parents' deaths."

"I know," he said. "I did terrible things. There is no reason for you to trust me. I wouldn't trust me either. But think how many more people could lose their families if we don't get off this island and stop Stalag."

Odette listened only briefly to his words before cutting him off. "Nope. See this?" Odette drew her foot across the sand, making a long indentation. "That is my line in the sand. There are some things, no matter how logical they may be, that I can never do. Helping the Infernal King is one of those things."

"I suppose a line is a line. If you all feel that way, we should just continue on our separate paths." Kestrel pulled out a satchel of mussels from his bag. "But if you happen to be hungry, I can't possibly eat all these myself."

Wily could feel his stomach grumble at the thought of food. Yet no matter how hungry he was, he would never accept food from his father, never mind dine with him.

"I should thank you for collecting the firewood," Kestrel said as he put the mussels in the flames.

"If we had known the fire was yours," Odette replied, "we would have let it go out."

"Is she always this cranky?" Kestrel asked Wily.

"The prisonaut was too good for you," Odette spat back.

Kestrel sat down by the now-raging fire and rotated the mussels with a stick.

"I know how to build a boat," Kestrel said. "I've done it before. Can you?"

"Wily built an engine from scratch once," Roveeka said. "And a mechanical bird."

"He is quite skilled with metal and gears," Kestrel said. "But I know how to carve and bend wood. Waterproof it. It was a hobby I had before Wily was born. I'm sure in a few years you all will figure it out on your own, but right now, you might need a little help."

"I don't need your help," Wily said, even though he

felt foolish saying it, because his father was right: he had never built anything from wood. Then he turned to his companions. "Let's go."

Odette didn't need much convincing. She was already walking down the beach. The rest of the group followed her, walking quickly across the hot sand. Wily continued away from his father's camp, marching swiftly without looking back. Once they had made it past the next outcropping, Pryvyd raised his hand to the others.

"Let's talk," Pryvyd said.

"About what?" Odette said, still fuming.

Pryvyd held his shoulders high and took a long calm breath before speaking again.

"I hate him more than anyone in Panthasos," Pryvyd said. "For what he did to you, Odette. And what he did to Wily. And Lumina. And all of Panthasos. Removing his head from his shoulders would be well deserved."

"Couldn't agree more," Odette said. "I'll help sharpen the sword."

"But I also know that working with a snake is better than being bitten by one," Pryvyd said. "He has knowledge that we lack. We need his help to build a boat swiftly."

"Are you crazy?" Odette nearly screamed. "He's the Infernal King!"

"We can't get off this island as fast without him," Pryvyd said.

"Remember that line I drew in the sand?" Odette

asked. "I'm still not crossing it. He is the one responsible for my parents' deaths."

"And Stalag could be responsible for many more families being split apart if we don't stop his new plans. Just think about how close he was with the army of stone golems."

"Just because you're the oldest one here, it doesn't make you the wisest. I can see that concerned fatherly look you are trying your best to pull off. But it won't change my mind."

Moshul used his large, muddy hands to push Odette and Pryvyd, who were now practically nose to nose, apart from each other.

"I am trying to be responsible," Pryvyd explained. "Take my emotions out of this decision. Because I do care about you."

"I liked you better when you were acting more like a reckless explorer and less like a parent." Odette crossed her arms in a huff.

As his two companions argued, questions shot through Wily's mind like darts in the blowgun tunnel. *How long will it take to learn how to build boats of wood? Can we wait that long with all the horrible things that Stalag is planning? I need to get back, warn Mom, and help her prepare for his army's arrival. But working with my father? Is anything worth that?* Then his mother's face flashed in his mind. Then Valor's face. Then all the people of Panthasos staring up at him in the royal palace tower.

"Think of all the gearfolk, snagglecarts, and pris-onauts that Stalag and his fellow cavern mages might have already rebuilt," Pryvyd said. "The Infernal King's machines enhanced by magic would be more than they could handle without our help."

"The boat he'll help us build will sink in the Eversteel Sea, " Odette said. "And he'll be smiling while we drown."

Roveeka walked over and gave Wily a gentle tap on the hand.

"He's your father," Roveeka said to Wily. "What do you think we should do?"

Odette, Pryvyd, Moshul, and Righteous turned to hear his response. Wily looked out at the waves rolling up onto the beach, considering what to say next.

"I agree with Odette . . ."

Odette smirked, satisfied.

". . . and Pryvyd."

And then Odette gave a loud huff of displeasure.

"We need Kestrel's help to get off this island," Wily continued. "But I don't trust him. Not at all."

"So what does that mean?" Odette asked.

Wily explained his plan to the rest of them.

"If we do this," Odette said, already despising the words coming from her lips, "we must never let Kestrel out of our sight."

"Understood," Wily said. "We have two companions who never sleep." Moshul nodded and Righteous gave a thumbs-up. "We will be able to keep our eyes on him. Sometimes it is better to keep your enemies close."

"I can't believe any of you are agreeing to this," Odette said to Pryvyd, fury in her eyes.

"Remember, we all want the same thing," Pryvyd said.

Wily took heavy steps back down the beach to the campfire, where his father was flipping mussels on the cooking stone. His companions walked behind him.

"Have you changed your mind?" Kestrel asked, his lips upturned into a slight smile. "Are we working together?" Kestrel stretched his legs out so that his shoeless toes nearly touched the flames, and he locked his hands behind his head. As he waited expectantly for Wily to reply, he jabbed one of the baked mussels with his roasting stick and lifted it into the air. He snatched it in his delicate fingers, cracked the shell open wider, and popped the fleshy innards into his mouth. He chewed on it slowly as he twirled the roasting stick in his hand.

"No," Wily said. "We are not working together. You are working for us."

Moshul approached Kestrel as Righteous flew over and grabbed him by the shoulder.

"What are you doing?" Kestrel said with alarm.

Moshul snapped off a stretch of thick vines from his body and began to tie them around Kestrel's wrists.

"You will be our prisoner until you earn our trust," Wily explained.

"If you earn our trust," Odette added. "Because otherwise the vines stay on. Forever."

"And if I refuse this arrangement?" Kestrel asked as Moshul tightened the bonds on his wrists.

"I'm really hoping you do," Odette said. "Because I would love to see how deep you would sink with—"

"I suggest you help us," Pryvyd said, trying to maintain a sense of control. "You don't want me to let her loose on you."

Odette narrowed her eyes. Kestrel considered, glancing at Wily as he did.

"I will help you build the boat," Kestrel answered. "And you will see, in time, that I am now on your side."

"So what do we need to make this raft?" Odette said curtly. "Wood?"

"Not a raft," Kestrel countered. "A small sailing vessel. A raft would never make it to the next island. We will need a boat that we can steer. Look here." Kestrel gestured to a pile of large branches resting by his lean-to. "These are branches from the rubber trees up on the ridge." He lifted one in his now-bound hands and bent it gently. "They are flexible enough to bend and mold. I am only able to carry a few back at a time, but your moss golem is strong enough to take the whole forest."

"Moshul has a name," Roveeka said. "Not just 'moss golem.'"

Kestrel bowed his head apologetically. "My pardons to you, Moshul. If you can get enough to cover this whole beach, we should have enough to execute my plans."

Moshul looked up at the ridge and nodded.

"I'll go with you," Odette said before leading the moss golem off toward the hillside with the rubber trees.

Kestrel turned back to the remaining members of the group. "The rest of you can help me make the sealing wax. It will keep the pieces of wood together and prevent the boat from sinking. We wouldn't want to be out at sea and find ourselves suddenly taking on water."

"What do we make the wax out of?" Roveeka asked.

"That's the tricky part, little hobgoblet," Kestrel said.

10

HORSETRAP

"Why do I have a feeling I'm not going to like what you're going to say next?" Pryvyd asked.

"We need the pollen from the horsetrap plant," Kestrel said. "It's incredibly sticky and, when mixed with water, it will make a thick and powerful sealant."

"A horsetrap plant?" Pryvyd looked very uncertain. "Have you actually seen one on the island?"

"Not just seen." Kestrel chuckled grimly. "I nearly got swallowed whole by one. I was very clumsy. Should have seen the vines snaking around my ankles."

"Am I the only one who doesn't know what a horsetrap plant is?" Roveeka asked.

"Actually, I've never heard of them either," Wily said.

"You know that flytrap plant in the palace garden?" Pryvyd said. "Well, it's like that, only bigger. Much bigger, and much quicker too. Many a Knight of the Golden

Sun have lost their stallions to the vile plant while riding through the jungle of the Western Peninsula."

"And this pollen," Wily asked. "Where is it on the plant?"

"Inside the flower, of course," Kestrel said. "Where all pollen is. Didn't Stalag teach you any biology while you were in Carrion Tomb for all those years?"

"Actually," Wily answered, "I was too busy building traps and cleaning up the leftovers of the hapless adventurers that got caught in them to even learn how to—"

"And if you are wondering," Kestrel continued on, "if the flower is close to the horsetrap's mouth, the answer is a most resounding . . . yes. Hence my difficulty in getting it."

"I bet Righteous could fly in and get it without any problem," Roveeka said, giving the floating arm a nudge with her elbow.

"Not likely," Kestrel replied. "Even for a floating ghostly arm. The horsetrap plant only allows butterflies and bees to fly near without swallowing them up."

"If Lumina was here," Wily said, "she could have quelled a whole pack of butterflies and sent them in for the pollen."

"Yes," Kestrel said with a flicker of melancholy. "Your mother was always quite good with the little bugs and such."

"Unfortunately, she never got a chance to teach me that

trick," Wily said angrily. "Maybe if I hadn't been separated from her my entire life because of *you*, I would have been able to do the same. Then again, if I hadn't been separated from her, we wouldn't have had any of these problems."

"I told you that I have a lot of regrets about what I did," Kestrel said. "I'm trying to make up for it now."

"I don't believe a word you're saying."

"I can't prove it to you if we all remain stuck here on this island," Wily's father said.

"So how do you propose we get the pollen?" Wily asked. "I'm not a bird or butterfly queller."

"You built a giant mechanical bird to break into my Infernal Fortress," Kestrel stated. "Perhaps we can build a mechanical butterfly together? Not a huge one. One the size of a small kite. We could attach it to a string and fix a small mechanical scooper to the front to snatch the pollen."

"That sounds very risky," Pryvyd said.

"All the machine needs to do is fool a plant with very limited eyesight," Kestrel said. "It can see shapes and motion but not much else." Kestrel stood and picked up one of the rubber-tree branches in his bound hands. He used one end to begin drawing in the sand. Wily watched as his father quickly sketched out the blueprint of a kite with wings on hinges. Wily was impressed by the swiftness of his father's design work, but he immediately noticed a few structural flaws.

"How do you plan on flapping the wings without metal springs or mechanical pistons?" Wily asked, pointing to the lower side of the butterfly blueprint.

"I can see you have the brain of a master trap-smith," Kestrel replied. "It's a fine question, but one for which I already have an answer. Which is why we are going to collect those slender reeds near the tide pools." Wily looked over his shoulder at the yellow-hued shoots growing from the small pools of water at the top of the beach. Kestrel continued, "They are hollow inside."

Wily caught on quickly. "You're going to blow air through them to move the wings."

"We will make our own bellows just like the kind that would stoke the flames of a furnace, and connect them to the base of the mechanical butterfly with interconnected reeds."

"The air will push the wings up and gravity will pull them back down," Wily said. "It would look a lot like a butterfly." *A very clever idea*, Wily thought.

"I'll need your nimble fingers and fine eyesight to pull it off," Kestrel said. "My hands are too big to tie the reeds to the wings, especially without my glasses. The frames rusted away, leaving me with just the lenses. We need to do this together."

"Will it even work, though?" Pryvyd asked.

Both Wily and Kestrel nodded in unison and tilted

their chins in the exact same fashion. It was a detail that didn't go unnoticed by Wily and made him very uncomfortable.

The floating arm tapped Pryvyd on the shoulder and pointed to the tide pools.

"Righteous will go get the reeds," Pryvyd said, as the arm drifted off.

"Wily, do you have any tools left that have not fallen victim to the salt fog?" Kestrel asked.

Wily pulled the various wrenches, a screwdriver, and a hammer from his belt. It didn't take long to examine each.

"No," Wily said. "Everything has rusted."

"But I do," Roveeka said. "Mum and Pops are as sharp as ever."

Kestrel raised a curious eyebrow. Then whispered quietly from the side of his mouth, "Has she gone mad?"

"They're the names of her knives," Wily said as Roveeka handed Pops over to him.

"Oh, that makes sense," Kestrel replied. "I used to name my wrenches when I was a kid."

Wily found the thought of the Infernal King doing anything of the sort bizarre. *He is an evil tyrant! There is nothing relatable about him.*

"Start cutting this bark in strips this thick." Kestrel held his fingers a small distance apart. "Then we will fold the pieces together."

Over the next hour, Wily worked constructing the

mechanical butterfly as his father barked orders. He hated every minute of it.

oOo

KESTREL LED WILY, Righteous, Pryvyd, and Roveeka through the jungle holding the newly built machine in his still-bound hands. Wily was surprised by just how familiar his father seemed to be with the island, for having spent such a short time there. How had his father built traps, come up with a plan of escape, and explored the island all in about one day? Was he really that industrious, or was there something Wily didn't know?

Kestrel stopped by a palm tree and pulled one of his eyeglass lenses from his pocket. He put it up to his eye and examined a set of markings on the side of the tree.

"This way," Kestrel said, making a turn to the right.

The underbrush grew denser as the air grew sweeter. A powerful fragrance wafted through the tangle of leaves. It was as sweet as sprinkled sugar on the top of a cookie but with a much fruitier aroma, like a peach from the palace orchard that had been left out in the sun for too long.

As they walked closer to the smell, Wily could see an oversize melon hanging from a tree branch. Its prickly outside was cracked slightly, letting its golden center twinkle in the light. It appeared delicious.

"The sundropricot looks like the tastiest fruit you've ever put in your mouth," Kestrel said as he gestured to the hanging fruit. "And it is. Of course it is also bait for the horsetrap plant. Beneath is the largest pair of teeth you've ever seen."

Just then, a furry tree rat went bounding from branch to branch. Wily watched with trepidation as the rodent approached the area with the sundropricot. As soon as the furry tree rat spotted the golden fruit, it took off as fast as it could in the opposite direction. "Even the tree rats are far too smart to try to steal fruit from the horsetrap plant."

"Then why are we?" Roveeka asked fearfully.

Kestrel ignored her. "Now, do you see the white flower sitting just past the fruit? That's where we need to get the mechanical butterfly to." Wily's father bent down and began setting up the butterfly and the bellows. The bellows (which was kind of like an accordion crossed with a foot pump) sent air through the two thin reed tubes that ran along the sides of the kite string up to the wings of the mechanical butterfly.

"It would help greatly if you untied my hands," Kestrel said, looking up to the others. "Just until we get this pollen."

Pryvyd looked to Wily, who nodded his approval. Pryvyd leaned down to loosen the bindings on Kestrel's wrists. Once freed, Kestrel was able to manipulate the butterfly more easily.

"I will pump the air to the wings," Kestrel said to Wily. "And you will need to fly the butterfly like a kite."

"I've never flown a kite," Wily answered pointedly. "I was too busy being trapped in a dungeon feeding crab dragons and imprisoning adventurers. Plus, there isn't a lot of wind in tombs."

"Not true," Kestrel said. "There are cave drafts. I'm surprised that Stalag didn't teach you how to fly a kite in one of the bigger caverns. I explicitly instructed him to treat you like his own son."

"Yeah, I don't think he read the scroll with that instruction on it," Wily snapped back. "Or he has a very different conception of raising a son than anybody else. I was treated horribly by him."

"All the more reason to get our just revenge on the brittle old mage," Kestrel said, pretending that Wily's anger wasn't directed at him. "Now hold the string and allow the wind carry the winged machine back and forth. If we let the string out gradually, the plant shouldn't realize it's not a typical insect. Then once we get the butterfly to the flower, the tiny wooden blade should snap the stamen off and we can quickly tug the butterfly back with the pollen."

"Won't that hurt the plant?" Roveeka asked.

"Very possibly," Kestrel said. "Which is why we'll all want to be prepared to run away very quickly. Who knows how long the plant's vines stretch?"

"This seems very risky," Pryvyd stated as Righteous gestured in agreement.

"If you have a better way to get off this island," Kestrel replied, "I am happy to hear your suggestions."

Pryvyd remained silent as Kestrel rhythmically stomped down on the bellow, sending puffs of air shooting through the long, thin tubes. The butterfly's wings began to flap just like those of a real one.

Wily held on to the string as the mechanical insect took flight. With each pump on the bellows, the butterfly bobbed forward. As it neared the fruit, Wily thought that for a moment he could see the leaves begin to shift. But if the horsetrap plant was there, it did not show itself. The butterfly passed by the fruit and got closer to the flower. Wily delicately attempted to steer the machine onto the edge of the blossom. With some careful flying, he thought he would be able to land the butterfly directly on a petal.

Then, almost by sheer chance, the butterfly found its target. The curved stick jutting out from the butterfly's head was just a few inches from the stamen of the flower.

"Now, son," Kestrel said, "snap the stamen off and get the pollen."

Wily took a deep breath and pulled a secondary string. The small wooden blade at the tip of the tongue stick sliced a clean cut, lopping off the delicate center of the flower. The pollen fell into the small receptacle attached to the front of the butterfly.

At once, all the vines around the flower and fruit began to writhe as if in anger and pain.

"Pull the butterfly back in!" Kestrel yelled. "We can't lose the pollen!"

Suddenly, it seemed as if the whole jungle floor had opened up and become a giant mouth. Huge green, thorny teeth chomped upward, trying to snag the flying contraption out of the air. Wily tugged on the string hard, no longer concerned about whether it fluttered gently like a butterfly. The jaws missed their target but only by a finger's length. The horsetrap's eyestalks followed the butterfly.

"Bring it back faster!" Kestrel shouted.

Wily tugged again as the jaws of the horsetrap plant were launched into the air. This time, the jaws overshot the butterfly. Instead of chomping down on the machine itself, it snapped the strings and reeds that were attached to it, severing them instantly. The butterfly dropped to the jungle floor in a lifeless heap.

"You fool!" Kestrel screamed. "That was our best and only chance at getting off the island!"

Wily wanted to scream back at his father, but at this very moment, all he cared about was getting the bundle of pollen. He wanted to get off the island even more than his father did.

"I'll get it," Wily said.

"No," Roveeka called out. "Did you see those teeth? Super sharp!"

Pryvyd grabbed Wily by the shoulder before he could move for it.

"You're not going in there," Pryvyd said. "No one is. We'll find another way."

While Pryvyd was speaking, Righteous took off. It flew toward the downed butterfly with its ghostly hand outstretched.

"Won't anyone listen to me?" Pryvyd shouted.

Righteous was swift. Its hand grabbed the wooden kite in its pale fingers as arm and elbow spun around. Before Righteous got far, though, one of the horsetrap's vines whipped around its wrist. The arm was tugged backward toward the now open mouth of the killer plant.

"We need to get out of here," Kestrel said. "Before a whole jungle of vines surround us."

"And leave my arm behind?" Pryvyd said, now furious.

"Well, it's not attached to your body anyway," Kestrel retorted. "Is it really such a loss?"

"You're lucky I don't feed you to the plant," Pryvyd said. He turned to Roveeka. "I need to borrow Mum!" he said, and she tossed him the knife without hesitation.

As Pryvyd ran for the mouth of the plant, he punched and kicked away the slithering vines that were surrounding him from all sides.

"I'm coming for you, Righteous," the Knight of the Golden Sun called to his arm.

Wily looked at the mechanical butterfly lying on the jungle floor. It was not too far away. With just a few steps, he could snatch it up himself. He hesitated, wondering what he should do. As he was lost in thought, a vine shot out from the underbrush and wrapped around his ankle. With a powerful pull, it tugged him toward the open mouth of the horsetrap.

"Wily!" Roveeka shouted.

Wily's hands scrabbled to find something to grab hold of, a root or rock wedged into the ground. As he turned around, he saw Kestrel moving in his direction. His father reached out. Wily stretched his arm toward him. His father grabbed—the mechanical butterfly off the ground.

The two, father and son, made eye contact. Then Kestrel quickly looked away, and Wily was pulled farther toward the mouth, the prickly jaws of which were wide open, ready for a meal.

WHOOSH. Mum sliced past Wily's ear. Pryvyd, holding the knife, slashed the vine that was tugging Wily into the mouth, cutting it clean in half. Righteous tugged Wily off the ground and pulled him away from the mouth, which snapped out as far as its roots could stretch. One of the thorny teeth snagged onto Wily's trapsmith belt, but he would not let himself be caught a second time. He pulled himself free and heard the leather band snap in two. Righteous grabbed the precious belt before it hit the ground, and the three of them ran and flew out of range of the plant.

As soon as they were safely away from the horsetrap plant, Wily turned to Kestrel, rage in his eyes.

"You saved the pollen," he shouted, "but didn't bother to reach for your own son?"

"I could see that Pryvyd was going to save you," Kestrel said without a hint of malice in his voice. "Just like he did."

"You would have rather let me be swallowed whole by the plant," Wily spat, "than lose the gunk that is going to get you off the island."

"I can tell you're very upset," Kestrel said. "And rightfully so. You have just been through a very traumatic experience. But you are completely misreading the situation."

"That's not how I see it. Tie his wrists up again."

Without argument, Kestrel held his hands out for Pryvyd to bind him.

"Then we can agree to disagree," Kestrel said as he headed back off through the jungle, clutching the mechanical butterfly in his tied hands. Wily could feel his blood boiling over like lava pouring down the sides of a volcano.

11

NIGHT WATCHING

"There you are," Odette called to Wily, who was following Kestrel back to the campfire. "You left us here with all the hard work while you were off picking flowers."

"Something like that," Wily said. He certainly didn't want to tell Odette what had actually happened. It had been hard enough convincing her to use Kestrel's assistance. He could only imagine what she would think if she learned how his father had nearly gotten Wily eaten.

Moshul and Odette sat on the soft sand splitting the trunks of the rubber trees into long, flat slices. The moss golem peeled them apart with ease, like pulling the stringy bits out of a piece of cooked celery. Odette was arranging them flat on the sand to bake them in the sun. Wily's father stopped before the stretch of wood slices laid out on the ground.

"They need to be even," he said. "And much thinner. We will need them to be pliable enough to bend. Keep them in the shade."

"Since you know how to do it right and we clearly don't, why don't you do it yourself?" Odette suggested petulantly.

"I'm afraid this will make that tough," Kestrel retorted, lifting his hands. "Golem, we need to soak these planks in salt water. Follow me. Hurry up!"

As Moshul dragged a dozen boards down to the sea, Wily sat next to Odette to help her finish peeling the bark off a wood slice.

"No wonder he built an army of mechanical people," Wily said. "Regular folk would never tolerate being treated like mindless workers."

"He's worse than just bossy," Odette said. "I fear for our own safety."

"You don't need to convince me."

Over the next six hours, Wily didn't let his father out of his sight, even if he was being watched by someone else. When Kestrel went to the stream in the jungle for a drink of water, Wily was thirsty too. When his father needed more shale to sand the insides of the planks, Wily volunteered to go with him. Kestrel always put on a good face, claiming he was happy for the help or company, but as he turned away, Wily often thought he noticed a sneer or an eye roll of exasperation from his father. Wily's caution ensured that there was never a moment when his father had a chance to sabotage Wily's friends' safety.

By midnight, the small sailboat was three-quarters finished. Kestrel had bossed everyone around as if he still were the Infernal King, telling them how to properly use the sealing wax and where to apply it for maximum effect. He instructed Pryvyd and Righteous on how to weave a small sail out of palm leaves. Wily had examined the sail upon completion. He concluded that although it was not as agile and impressive as one made from cloth, it would at least help the ship to travel slowly across the sea. Wily's eyes were getting tired as the night continued, but he fought sleep with every droop of his lids. It was hard for him to tell if he'd nodded off occasionally, but by the extreme exhaustion he was feeling by dawn, he had a strong hunch that he had managed to stay awake. Moshul and Righteous had never stopped building the boat, even when everyone else had dozed off under the stars.

As the sun came up over the jungle trees, Wily looked to see what progress had been made. To his surprise, he realized that all that was left to do was to push the boat into the sea. Kestrel placed his few belongings into it.

"Are you sure the boat will float?" Pryvyd asked Kestrel as he inspected the sides of the vessel.

"What I build never fails," Kestrel said without a lick of doubt. "Everyone get aboard."

Pryvyd did not seem so keen on heading out to sea again.

"Try to keep your food in your belly," Odette said.

"What food?" Pryvyd asked. "We've barely eaten in days."

"That might be a good thing after how green you turned on the *Coal Fox*." Odette snickered with her typical morning-elf spunk.

Kestrel was the first to climb in. All but Moshul followed, taking seats on the benches built into the boat. The moss golem pushed the craft down the beach into the water. To everyone's delight, especially Pryvyd's, the boat floated gently without a single leak. Moshul pulled himself aboard as Righteous raised the leaf sail.

"If we head around to the north," Pryvyd said, "we can circle the island and sail back to Panthasos."

"Or we could go west from here," Kestrel replied.

"What are you talking about?" Odette asked. "That's the opposite direction of Panthasos."

"We could go to Drakesmith Island," Kestrel said. "And find the Eversteel Forge."

"Nobody knows if it even exists," Pryvyd replied, "let alone where on the island it is hidden."

"I've been collecting clues for years," Kestrel said. "I am certain that once we explore the island we will be able to make sense of them. If we follow those stars to the west, we could reach Drakesmith by dawn."

"The reason we built the ship," Pryvyd clarified,

"was to go back and aid Lumina in defending the royal palace."

"I've seen the enchanted gearfolk," Kestrel said. "Lumina and her ferrets won't stand a chance against them. So unless you plan on trying to recruit Palojax again, you're—or rather—*we're* going to need another solution. I say we find the forge and build the new uber-gearfolk I designed to fight *against* Stalag rather than *for* him."

"This wasn't part of the deal," Pryvyd said. He turned to Wily. "What do you think?"

"We go back to Panthasos," Wily said. "That's not going to change."

"Suit yourself," Kestrel said with more than a hint of disapproval.

HOURS OF THE boat rocking with each small wave made resisting taking a nap extremely challenging for the very weary Wily. Yet he knew it was far more important to keep his eyes trained on Kestrel. Wily tried to find small patches of shade to keep his skin from crisping, but besides Moshul's towering body and the triangle of palm leaves attached to the mast, there were few places to hide from the sun's blistering rays.

As the sun set to the west, the temptation to sleep grew even more difficult to resist. He watched as Righteous gently glided the rudder, making small shifts in the boat's direction. He could hear Roveeka snoring beside him. On his other side, Odette was running in her sleep, just the way a baby scorpion would try to sting imaginary prey while it was dozing.

Plop. Wily heard a soft splash. He turned just in time to see Kestrel pull his hand away from the water. *What was that about?*

"Did you just drop something into the water?" Wily asked, looking his father straight in the eye.

"I have no idea what you are talking about," Kestrel replied as Pryvyd peeked his eyes open.

"Yes, you do," Wily said. "Just now, I heard a—"

CRAAACK. Everyone in the boat lurched forward as the boat made contact with something hard. Then came the sound of rushing water. Wily turned to the front of the boat. Between Roveeka and Pryvyd a sharp rock was jutting out through the cracked hull. Seawater was rapidly flooding the bottom of the vessel.

"We've run aground!" Kestrel shouted.

"You did something to cause it," Wily screamed as he leaped to his feet.

"Why would I damage a ship I was sitting in? That makes no sense."

"I'm sure you have a reason."

"You're looking for reasons not to trust me," Kestrel said. "How could I make a giant rock appear in the middle of the ocean?"

"None of this arguing will stop the water from

pouring in!" Pryvyd screamed as he began scooping sea-water out of the boat with his hand.

"Untie me," Kestrel said. "Let me help."

"No!" Wily, Odette, and Pryvyd screamed in unison.

"I don't want to be stranded on a rock in the middle of the ocean," Roveeka said. "We've already done it once and it wasn't particularly fun."

Moshul was signing and pointing into the distance.

"There's an island over there," Odette translated for Moshul.

"Good spotting, Moshul," Pryvyd said. "If we can push off the rock, we may be able to make it to shore. Give me some help over here."

Righteous, Odette, and the moss golem joined Pryvyd at the front of the boat. All four leaned over and started pushing with all their might. It seemed as if they were struggling.

"Everyone get on the right side of the boat," Odette shouted back to Wily, Roveeka, and Kestrel. "We might be able to shake it loose."

Wily slid over so he was pressed up against Roveeka. Kestrel did the same as they tried to tip the ship.

"This is cozy," Roveeka said, squished against the side of the boat. She looked into the water and brightened. "We're moving!"

Surprised, Wily peered over to see that Roveeka was dipping her fingers into the water. Sure enough, a trail of water followed the path of her fingers. The boat seemed to be moving.

"We can't be moving!" Pryvyd called back. "We're still stuck on the rock."

Wily spun forward to see that Pryvyd was correct too.

"That's impossible," Wily said. "Unless the rock is moving too."

"Or unless we're not stuck to *a rock*," Odette said.

Moshul let a swarm of fireflies take flight from his palm. They swooped down and lit the small portion of ocean in front of the boat. Wily could now see that the spike that pierced the front of the boat was actually just one of many spikes attached to a giant shell three times larger than the boat. Wily looked to the front of the shell, where an elongated head with red eyes and a pointed nose stared back at him.

"It's a turtle dragon," Odette said in a hushed scream. "The largest one I've ever seen."

"I told you I didn't crash into it on purpose," Kestrel whispered to Wily. "How could I have known where a turtle dragon would be?"

"You lured it using some kind of bait," Wily said. "That's what you were dropping in the ocean."

Kestrel gave Wily a withering stare. "How would that help me? Remember, I'm in the same boat as you."

"Save the arguing for later!" Pryvyd called back to the father and son.

The turtle dragon lifted its mouth to the sky and let out an angry croak that shook the air. It turned its neck so it could bite at the unwelcome visitors. Fortunately, unable to reach the boat at the very back of its shell, the dragon let out another loud grunt.

"I'm sorry to be pointing out the obvious," Odette said, panic rising in her voice, "but if the turtle dragon decides to dive and the boat is still stuck on its spikes, we're all going to drown."

Before there was a time to come up with a plan, Moshul leaped off the boat and onto the shell of the turtle dragon. This seemed to both confuse and surprise the creature, which started snapping at Moshul. The moss golem punched the turtle in the nose, stunning it for a moment. There was little time. Moshul turned back to the boat and used his massive strength to lift it off the spike. With a heaving toss, he threw the boat back into the water, setting it on a course for the island in the distance. The turtle dragon snapped at Moshul again, biting a clump of mud from his shoulder. Moshul then took a running dive off the turtle dragon's shell. With a huge splash, the golem went underwater and surfaced right behind the boat.

Wily watched as the turtle dragon gave a puzzled look before paddling off toward deeper waters, seemingly happy to be rid of the pesky land dwellers. Moshul wrapped his hands over the back edge of the boat and began kicking it toward the island.

"Keep kicking," Roveeka said to Moshul with an encouraging smile.

Odette eyed the hole in the boat, which was taking on water even faster now that it wasn't partially plugged by the turtle dragon's spike.

"And kick fast!"

12

PAINFUL BITES

The group dragged the leaky boat up onto the sandy beach of the island they had made landfall on. Even in the dark of night, Wily could see that this island was quite different from the one they had previously been stranded on. The beach was made of black sand dotted with amethyst boulders. There were no trees (screaming or otherwise) to be seen, only tall grass that was higher than Wily's head. Even the small crabs that scurried across the sand looked nothing like the ones that had tried to make a home in Wily's locks. The small crustaceans each had one giant claw and one that was tiny. The island smelled different too. The scent of sweet fruit mixed with dried kelp sat heavy in the air.

"This doesn't look promising," Kestrel said, examining the damage to the boat.

"We have plenty of extra sealing wax," Odette said, holding up a shell full of the sticky substance.

"But we will need new planks to patch this up," Kestrel pointed out, "and I don't see any trees to get wood from."

Wily looked back at the island and realized he was right.

"Maybe there's some on the far side of the island," Roveeka said hopefully.

"We'll be able to see better when the sun comes up in a few hours," Kestrel said.

He took a seat in the sand, pressed his back up against the wooden hull of the boat, and closed his eyes. The rest of the group found spots to rest as well. Wily was certainly not going to sleep at all. He had already caught his father doing strange things while others were sleeping. He couldn't let him get away with doing anything else. But despite watching Kestrel until the break of dawn, or perhaps because of it, his father didn't do anything else suspicious.

As the sky began to change colors with the coming of the sun, Wily heard a low hum. The sound was similar to the noise the rot flies would make when they swarmed in circles around the leftover meat decomposing on the cave floor. Only this noise was much louder, and getting louder with every second. Wily looked around to see what was responsible for the sound. Just then, he saw something whoosh overhead and land on his back. Before he could turn, he felt a sharp poke on his neck and a flash of intense pain.

"Ow!"

He turned to see a mosquito the size of a hummingbird perched on his shoulder. Its needle-like sucker was stuck deep into his flesh, slurping out blood.

"Get it off me!" Wily screamed, putting an end to everybody's slumber.

Righteous was the first to react. The arm shot forth, grabbed the bug in its ghostly fist, and tugged it free. Wily winced as the long poker was drawn from his skin.

"There's one on me too," Odette shouted. Wily turned to see that not one, but two had landed on Odette and were prodding her for a drink of blood.

"These horrid bugs want to suck us dry," Kestrel said.

"They don't seem interested in me," Roveeka said as one of the bloodsuckers flew right by her. "It must be my tough hobgoblet skin."

"Or maybe," Odette said as she tumbled in the sand to rid her back of the pests, "your blood tastes like mold juice."

"Can't be," Roveeka said. "If that were the case, I bet every single one of them would want to eat me."

Moshul batted the mosquitoes away from Pryvyd and Odette with the back of his muddy hand as they continued to swarm around the companions.

"Travelers from the mainland," an elegant voice rang out from the trees, "welcome to the Isle of Delight!"

Moments later, an entire party of beings was standing before them. It was impossible to tell what species they were because they were shrouded in layers of thin netting from the tops of their heads all the way down to their feet. It reminded Wily of the few times in Carrion Tomb when the residents dressed in bedsheets for the festival of Glothmurk and Wily could not tell who was who.

"Gaskar," the leader of the group continued with a gentle lilt, "shoo the vectrites away."

One of the shrouded locals placed a candle in the sand and lit it with a piece of flint stick. A thick cloud of pungent vapor rose from the smoking candle. The vectrites quickly scattered.

"They are vicious little bugs," the cloaked leader said.

"Not so little actually," Odette said.

"What good fortune brings you here?" he continued.

"Our ship was struck by a turtle dragon and sprang a leak," Wily said, pointing to the grounded vessel. "This island was the nearest piece of land."

"Oh, so you had an encounter with Prickleback," the voice replied from beneath the netting. "You're not the first. She's a very curious turtle dragon. Not a particularly cross gal, but she'll toss a ship just to watch the sailors scramble."

"If you don't mind me asking," Roveeka spoke up, "why are you wearing that net over your head?"

"To keep the vectrites away," the net-covered native said. "They can't get their suckers through the mesh. In the afternoon, they're pretty aggressive."

"Worse than the morning?" Pryvyd said, scratching a rapidly growing welt that was expanding at the bite point on his shoulder.

"That will be an itchy one," the netted leader said as he pulled the thin fabric up from his feet to above his head. "But as the philosophers say, the only true comfort is found in the mind."

Wily was shocked by what he saw underneath the net: webbed hands, spikes down the arms, and a head that resembled a fish's. This eloquent islander was an oglodyte.

"You're an oglodyte?" Wily asked more as a statement than a question.

"And you're very observant," the oglodyte said. "Why does it shock you so?"

Wily explained how the two oglodytes he knew best, Sceely and Agorop, were both dim-witted, unpleasant buffoons.

"I see," the oglodyte said. "Well, I'm happy to say that we're not all alike. My name's Jayrus. Of the Hammock oglodytes."

"You really are very different," Wily said.

"I am so embarrassed that those two are representing our kind poorly," Jayrus said. He then looked to the vessel. "Can I send my friends over to inspect the damage to your boat?"

A pair of the netted oglodytes stepped forward. Wily led them down to the edge of the water, where they proceeded to examine the ship. They surveyed the damage caused by Prickleback (although it was hard to imagine how they could see anything at all through the layers of white mesh).

"It's quite bad," one of Jayrus's companions said as she ran her hidden hand over the outside of the boat.

"Rotten indeed," another oglodyte concurred. "You won't be making it far with a hole like this."

"We need wood to patch it up," Kestrel said, lifting his hands so that the vines binding his wrists were visible. Jayrus looked over at the makeshift cuff suspiciously. Kestrel explained it away with a simple explanation. "I did something I shouldn't have done."

"We all make mistakes," Jayrus responded. "Now about that wood. I'm afraid all the trees were cut down this past spring. But we have plenty of nets back at the camp. You can live with us until the trees grow back. It shouldn't be more than thirty years or so."

"That's a very kind offer," Wily said. "But we plan on leaving here as soon as we can and continuing on our journey. We need to return to Panthasos."

"Why would you want to go back there?" Jayrus replied. "Last time someone stopped by from the mainland we heard it was being ruled by a truly horrible king wearing a helmet with three points."

Wily quickly turned to Kestrel, waiting to see his response. His father did not flinch at the description. Instead he spoke quite calmly. "It had been. But things have changed. Now it is ruled by kind people who would never cause harm to others. Unless a new evil mage takes over."

"Yes, well," Jayrus seemed to consider. "It sounds like a pretty mixed-up place, if you ask me. Glad I'm here and not there."

"We just need a few planks of wood," Wily said. "Perhaps you have some spare pieces we could have."

"Unfortunately, no," Jayrus said as he lowered the netting over his body again. "All the wood was used to build the ship moored in the hidden lagoon. We didn't need any of the wood ourselves so we let him have it."

"Wait . . . wait," Odette spoke up. "Did you say there is an already-built ship?"

"Yes," Jayrus said. "One large enough to sail a hundred across the deepest sea."

"We don't need to repair our boat," Odette said. "We would be happy to borrow the hidden ship in the lagoon."

"It doesn't belong to us," Jayrus explained slowly, as if speaking to a child, which in fact he was. "The ship is the property of the Recluself. He's a bit of a loner and doesn't associate with others."

"Tell us more about this Recluself," Kestrel said.

"He was the former engineer for the Brine Baron," Jayrus said. "During one of their sea journeys, he drank a little too much nectar and fell off his master's ship. He washed ashore many years ago, and our tribe rescued him. He was not a big fan of the vectrites, just like you are not. So he locked himself away in the caves with the scatbats, which have a real taste for the vectrites."

"And he built a boat?" Wily asked.

"As the former engineer of the Brine Baron," Jayrus explained, "he was quite good at putting things together on his own. In the years he has been down there, he has constructed the most beautiful vessel. And it is just sitting there, waiting to be sailed."

"Then why hasn't he left?" Odette asked.

"Don't know for sure," Jayrus replied. "And we haven't really asked. He doesn't like visitors. Thinks we might drag in vectrite eggs. He's locked up the place very tightly. Only once or twice have oglodytes been able to sneak in for a peek."

"Locked up the place with traps?" Kestrel asked.

"Very tough ones," Jayrus remarked. "Very hard to get past them."

"I think we have that covered," Roveeka said as she turned to both Wily and his father. "Doubly so."

Wily looked at his father skeptically as he used his

knuckles to scratch the ever-expanding bump on his shoulder.

"Please point us in the direction of the Recluself's cave," Pryvyd said.

"Of course," Jayrus said. "But I think you might want some nets before you go anywhere."

13

THE RECLUSELF

Wily felt as ridiculous as he looked. A wooden ring sat on his head with a dozen layers of thin netting hanging down from it. It felt like he was wearing a set of curtains. Fortunately, the mesh was thin enough that his vision wasn't completely clouded, but it did give everything in front of him a thick, milky glow. His human, hobgoblet, and elf companions also wore the vectrite-protective netting as they pushed through the jungle. It was lucky that Moshul didn't have blood to suck, because there was not enough netting in all of Hammock Town to cover his gigantic body. Even Pryvyd was too tall for the single nets they typically used. The helpful oglodytes had quickly sewn on an extra few inches of fabric so that the vectrites couldn't make a meal of his ankles.

Jayrus was whistling happily as he led the group toward the rocky peninsula that was home to the

Recluself's cave. They had been walking for the better part of an hour, passing through small creeks teeming with bugs, and prickly underbrush even more dense with insects. Wily had spent much of that time explaining to Jayrus and the other Hammock oglodytes what had happened to them since they left the royal palace eight days earlier. He also told them of all the horrible things Stalag had done in the past, but thought it best not to mention who Kestrel was.

Wily felt a boot kick in the calf from behind.

"My apologies, Roveeka," Pryvyd said. "Didn't mean to kick you. A bit hard to see where I am going."

"No problem," Roveeka said. "I didn't feel a thing."

"That's because he kicked me," Wily said.

"Whoops," Pryvyd replied. "Guess it's hard to see who's who as well."

Wily heard a loud thump followed by a noise that reminded him of mushrooms being squashed in a press. He turned to see Moshul in a panic. He was pointing to his leg and waving to the others.

Looking down, Wily spied a small tentacled creature clinging to Moshul's leg. It had big blue eyes like a gristle puppy and a happy expression on its face.

Help! Moshul signed.

"I'll give you a hand," Pryvyd said. "Just relax. Shouldn't take more than a moment, big guy."

"Oh," Jayrus said. "Lucky you! The hugtopus brings good luck."

Moshul was shaking his head.

"He's terrified of things with tentacles," Odette said. "He just wants it off."

"Easy enough." Jayrus said. "You'll just have to kill it."

Wily eyed the super cute creature. Moshul did too as he trembled.

"It's the only way," the oglodyte continued. "They only let go when they want to. Otherwise you need to stab it in the head with something sharp."

The hugtopus looked pleadingly up at Moshul.

Fine, the moss golem signed. *I will wait. Don't kill it.*

"No worries," Jayrus said. "The longest they cling to you is a mere two or three years."

Moshul's jeweled eyes looked ready to cry.

"That's it," Jayrus called out, pointing a shrouded hand at a large wooden door that looked particularly out of place in the stone wall that seemed to have sprouted from the jungle floor.

"I'm guessing it's locked," Odette said. "And it doesn't even look like it has a keyhole."

"It's bolted from the inside," Jayrus said. "As I mentioned, the Recluself doesn't come out much."

Wily looked to see that the stone hinges of the door were buried deep in the rock wall.

"Even if I had my screwdriver or arrowtusk lock picks," Wily said, "it would do little to help break in through this door."

"With a mechanical winch," Kestrel said, "we could pry it open."

"Luckily, we have something better," Pryvyd said. "We have a golem."

Pryvyd began signing to Moshul, who nodded and stepped up to the door. Moshul clenched his mud fist and punched the door. Despite the intense force, the door held fast, barely sustaining a dent.

"That's not how I thought this would go," Pryvyd said. "Try again."

Moshul swung even harder. This time the door splintered but still remained taut on its hinges. Wily saw out of the corner of his eye that Kestrel, hands still tied, had wandered off. He was approaching a portion of the stone wall that jutted out slightly from the rest of the surface.

"You, moss golem," Kestrel said. "Use your fist over here."

Moshul looked to Odette for approval. He signed, *Should I?*

Odette's netting shook up and down. "If you can't tell, I am nodding right now," Odette said. "Go ahead."

"One hard hit should do the trick," Kestrel said, pointing to a fracture point in the rock.

Moshul struck the spot with the side of his fist. A thin slab of rock cracked off the wall and slid to the ground. The chunk nearly fell on the hugtopus, which was still wrapped tightly around Moshul's leg.

"What good is that going to do?" Odette asked impatiently.

"I think I know what Kestrel is thinking," Wily said with a glimmer of hope. "Slide the tip of the stone into the gap between the bottom of the door and the ground. If a door has been hung on rock hinges, then it can also be lifted off them. Moshul, press down on the exposed portion of the rock."

Moshul smashed his foot down on the stone just as Wily had instructed. Like a fulcrum and lever, the other side of the rock moved upward, putting force on the bottom of the door. Sure enough, the door was lifted up and off its hinges. With a mighty crash, it fell forward toward the group, slamming into the ground.

"That's not good!" Odette said with a groan, looking past the toppled wooden door.

Wily followed her line of sight to see that just beyond was yet another wooden door seemingly just as thick.

"This guy really doesn't like his bugs," Odette said.

"I don't blame him," Wily said, swatting a vectrite by his head.

Moshul tossed the fallen door behind them and picked up the stone slab. He repeated the very same trick and dislodged the next door from its hinges too. Fortunately, there were no further doors that they could see.

"Thank you for the nets and guiding us here," Wily said to Jayrus and the other Hammock oglodytes.

"We're not going to let you go in there alone," Jayrus said. "We plan on helping you until you no longer need our assistance. We're oglodytes. We gaberflimp. That's what we do for each other. That's what we'll do for you."

"*Gaberflimp?*" Roveeka said.

"Ah yes," Jayrus explained. "We have thirty-two words that mean 'help.' *Gaberflimp* means 'to give assistance with no expectation of a favor in return.'"

"Absolutely nothing," Odette said. "That's what you have in common with mainland oglodytes."

"I'll take that as a compliment," Jayrus said.

"You have no idea," Wily said.

Jayrus and the other oglodytes took the rear as Wily and his companions entered the mouth of the cave. Inside, it was quite dark; only the few rays of sun from the outside kept it from being pitch-black. Wily was unimpressed. Even the most inhospitable dungeons should be lit properly. How else could invaders have a fair chance against traps? It was clear that the Recluself was not familiar with proper dungeon etiquette. Clearly, he had no desire for anyone to make it even this far.

As they continued inside, Wily discovered that there was more than just oglodytes following them. A persistent swarm of vectrites, still determined to get their lunch, buzzed circles around the netted heads of Odette and Wily. Wily was about to ask Jayrus to pull out one of the scented candles when he heard a loud *whoosh*, followed by a screech. Something large and black went flapping overhead. It was a giant bat. Wily ducked as the creature soared overhead again. But the winged rodent wasn't coming for them. Instead it was getting a meal of its own. The vectrites that had been overhead were gone. In the dark, Wily could hear the sound of the bats crunching on insects.

"You can have your hugtopus. I want to keep one of those as a pet," Roveeka said, "with their cute beady eyes and pointy teeth. So snuggable."

Through the dim, Wily could see the bat, which had broken vectrite legs and suckers sticking out of its blood-covered mouth. The bat was not cute at all, in his opinion, but he was certainly glad the bats were there.

"Let's keep moving," Kestrel said, taking the lead, the tunnel getting darker with every step.

Pryvyd asked Moshul to release his fireflies to light the way, but the moss golem refused, afraid that the insects might be an easy snack for the cloud of bats flapping overhead. Without the fireflies, the group had to continue on in near darkness as the stone cave sloped downward. As they progressed deeper, Wily thought he could hear a waterfall nearby. In fact, the water sounded very close. Too close.

TWANG-CLICK. Wily knew that sound. A foot accidentally triggering a trapdoor. The stone floor opened beneath Kestrel's feet, sending him falling into a swirling whirlpool. Wily's father was churned in circles by the swift-moving water. Before he was sucked down into the hole at the center of the whirlpool, Kestrel reached out with his bound hands, grabbing hold of the ledge between the stone floor and the hanging trapdoor. His trembling fingers were the only thing keeping the rapidly rushing water from sweeping him into the eye of the whirlpool.

Wily, who had been a few steps behind Kestrel, was still safely standing on solid ground. He looked down to see that his father's fingers were slipping from the intense force being exerted on them. There were only moments before Kestrel would be lost to the darkness. Wily flung himself to his belly and reached an arm out toward his father.

"Grab my hand!" Wily shouted over the gurgling water.

He wasn't a moment too soon either. Kestrel grabbed for his son when his hands slipped from the slick rock. Wily pulled with all his strength as the water tugged Kestrel toward the center of the whirlpool. Wily felt as if his arms might be torn out of his shoulder sockets. He looked into his father's eyes, the eyes that looked so much like his own, as he struggled to hoist him out. His father did not look like the cruel Infernal King. His father looked like a person full of fear and panic. Just when Wily thought he would not be able to hold him any longer, Moshul's strong arms pulled him and his father onto the stone floor of the sloping chamber.

"That was close," Roveeka said.

"As far as traps go," Kestrel said, "this one isn't very impressive."

"What are you talking about?" Wily said. "It nearly killed you!"

"Exactly," Kestrel said as he got to his feet. "*Nearly.* What good is a trap that only nearly kills you? If I had designed it, it would have done the job it was intended to do."

Wily didn't know how to respond to this. He waited for his father to thank him, but it didn't come.

"Let's move along," Kestrel said. "And keep your eye out for more sloppy traps. This Recluself is clearly in need of some sophistication."

As Kestrel inched his way along the narrow band of rock hugging the whirlpool trap, Wily couldn't help but stare at him incredulously. He was angry, not only at his father, but himself too. He had just saved the life of the man he hated most. And he hadn't hesitated even for a second and had acted purely on instinct. Foolish, regrettable instinct.

"I can't believe I just did that," Wily said quietly to Pryvyd beside him. "If it had been the reverse and I was dangling, he would have let me drop."

"Listen, Wily . . . ," Pryvyd whispered back.

"I know what you are going to say," Wily interrupted. "I did the right thing."

"Actually," Pryvyd confided, "next time, I was hoping you would be a little slower in your rescuing. I think

Kestrel could use a dunk in a pitch-black whirlpool." Pryvyd gave him a wink. "But we should move along. We don't want him getting too far ahead of us."

As the group continued down through the tunnel, Wily saw that Kestrel took much more cautious steps and ran his fingers along the curves in the walls, searching for traps. Between father and son, the group managed to avoid triggering a falling boulder or activating a floor set to fire out poisonous needles. Despite not seeing anyone, Wily had the sense they were being watched, perhaps from one of the hidden maintenance tunnels that almost certainly ran parallel to the main corridor.

As the downward-sloping tunnel flattened out, they reached another wooden door that appeared to have been hastily closed. There was no need to lift this barrier off its hinges. A simple push swung it wide open. On the other side of the door, Wily discovered a long hall painted with colors that were swirling in constant motion.

"It's just like the mural at Halberd Keep," Wily said.

He remembered how the colors had formed a picture that only he could see. It had shown him Stalag plotting the rise of the Infernal Golem and given him a clue to his enemy's plan, although he hadn't quite understood it at the time.

"This has been here since my ancestors came to the island," Jayrus said, "long before the Recluself made it his grotto. It shows the world beyond the island. We are happy on the Island of Delight and have never seen the benefit of peering into other folks' lives."

As Wily stared at the walls, a picture began to form. His heart beat fast as his mother's face came into focus. She looked frightened. As more of the mural took shape, he could see that Valor was by her side and they were in the middle of intense combat. Stalag stood on the drawbridge of the royal palace as gearfolk rolled into the atrium. Lumina and Valor were trying to fend them off, but there were dozens, each armed with an ax that looked to be made from smoke. Impish and Gremlin, Lumina's loyal ferret companions, were knocked aside by the magically assisted machines as they continued to attack the palace. Wily could feel his heart pounding as he watched his loved ones struggle. If only he could jump into the mural and teleport to his mother's side. Stalag laughed as he raised his hands and shot arrows of crackling energy at Lumina. She dodged out of the way, but the forces against her and Valor were too great. They tried to back away and escape, but they were cornered by gearfolk and a snagglecart. The rolling cage swallowed them up, leaving them trapped inside. Stalag was laughing as he approached the side of the snagglecart. The cavern mage turned to an enchanted gearfolk and spoke. While Wily could not hear what he said, he could read the words slipping out from the mage's gray, cracked lips: "Take them to the prisonaut and lock them away." Lumina and Valor stood defiantly, but Wily could see his mother was trembling.

"I'll save you," Wily called out to the wall.

The image disappeared into a swirl of colors, leaving Wily desperate for one last peek.

"I saw my mom and Valor in danger," Wily said, turning to the others.

"Fighting Stalag?" Pryvyd said with equal concern. "I did too."

"So did I," Odette said.

"And the danger is just as Kestrel described," Wily said. "He was telling the truth about that."

"Lumina could normally take down three gearfolk at a time," Pryvyd said. "But she couldn't with them. The gearfolk are far more powerful than before."

"What are we going to do?" Odette said, lost in thought. "Even with our help, it may not be enough."

Wily was wondering the very same thing. Seeing this had changed everything. They would need more to defeat Stalag and his fellow mages. Palojax, the great lair beast, was gone. How would they save the day this time?

"Up here," Kestrel called from the end of the hall.

Wily moved to where his father was standing. Before them was a huge underground grotto. Just as Jayrus had said, a majestic wooden sailing ship was floating in the protected waters of the cave. It was roughly the size of the *Coal Fox* and appeared to be made of polished wood of all colors and sizes. Wily could only imagine how many hours, months, and years it had taken for a single person to build it. He watched it rock gently as waves lapped through the mouth of the cave.

Wily's attention was drawn to the roof of the cavern. It appeared as if it was moving too. At first Wily thought it was the reflection of the rippling water below, but after a few moments of careful inspection, he realized he was staring not at a stone ceiling but rather hundreds of thousands of hanging bats.

"Out! Get out!" a voice called from the ship. "You'll bring them in. They probably followed you. Why couldn't you have just left me alone?"

"There are no vectrites on us," Wily shouted in response.

"One could be hiding in your clothes," the voice called. "Waiting to pop out and get me."

"Wouldn't your bats catch them?" Roveeka asked.

"Can't be sure. Don't want to take any chances."

"Your visitors are not oglodytes," Jayrus called out. "One is even an elf like you. Hear them out. You at least owe them that."

A figure appeared on the deck of the ship. Wily squinted and could see an elf with hair as blue as Odette's and ears just as pointy as hers. He was wearing well-pressed slacks and a starched shirt.

"Doesn't seem like you're a big fan of this island," Odette said.

"I hate everything about it," the Recluself said. "I'd have left a dozen years ago if I could."

"Does the ship not fit through the exit of the grotto?" Roveeka asked.

"Of course it would," the elf scoffed. "I was the Brine Baron's master engineer. I never would have made a mistake like that. I measured the exit with a ruler many times."

"Then why are you still here?" Wily asked. "Do you need people to help you sail?"

"I built it so that one person could sail it alone. All the ropes and sails have been automated with exact precision. I don't need anyone."

"So . . . ," Roveeka said.

"It's the Eversteel Sea keeping me here," the elf said. "The last time I was out there, I almost drowned. I barely made it to the shore alive."

"But you didn't . . . ," Roveeka replied.

"I can't go back out there," the elf said. "What if there is another storm? Or a tidal wave? What if I am knocked into the sea again? Once horrible. Always horrible."

"You should give the ocean a second chance," Kestrel said. "Everything and everyone deserves that." It didn't take Wily a second to understand that these last words were meant for him and not the Recluself.

"From my little experience," Jayrus said, "the sea can be quite lovely."

Roveeka interjected. "But I understand being scared. Lately, I haven't been feeling very brave at all."

"My brain knows the sea to be safe," the elf said, "but my heart is less sure. A lot less sure. I keep thinking about the waves crashing over my head and the turtle dragon that knocked me off my last ship."

"So you're just going to stay here?" Odette asked.

"I will wait here until I know I will be completely safe on the Eversteel Sea," the elf said.

"Nothing is completely safe," Odette said. "And besides, the adventure of the new is what keeps us alive. It's what keeps us moving forward. We all need to be hunting for our own treasure, so to speak, or we end up stuck in a cave. Waiting." Wily could see that those last words meant more to Odette than they might have to the Recluself.

"We want to borrow your ship," Pryvyd said. "We need to get off the island, no matter how safe or not it may be out on the ocean."

"And I think you should come with us," Odette said.

"I couldn't," the Recluself said.

"We can't force you," Odette said.

"Well . . . maybe you could. If you kidnapped me, I wouldn't have a choice."

"Is he asking us to take him captive?" Wily whispered to Pryvyd.

"He is indeed an unusual fellow," Jayrus answered from nearby.

"Stay where you are," Wily said. "We're stealing your ship."

"How dare you!" the Recluself cried. "If you want to get on board, take those rowboats to the ship. Then you can pull the ship out using the cave pulleys."

The elf pointed to a trio of small-oared skiffs pulled up onto the cave floor.

"Even an automated ship," Jayrus said, "needs a crew. We could all use an adventure. We will join you. Besides, after what you saw on the wall, it sounds like you need us."

The other oglodytes all nodded under their nets as they boarded one of the three rowboats.

Wily and his companions boarded the other pair of rowboats and rowed their way out to the grand sailing vessel.

"Hurry up," the Recluself said. "The tides are in our favor." Then his voice changed to one of panic. "Actually, get away from me. Go back from where you came." Then he changed his mind once more. "Then again, I couldn't stand another night here."

A rope ladder made it an easy climb aboard. When Wily got on deck, he was surprised by just how much attention had been paid to it. The Recluself might have been a terrified man, but he was also a master crafts-man. He was sitting on the deck with his hands held over his head. Roveeka sat down to try to calm him.

"It's a very beautiful ship," she said. "Does it have a name?"

"Never bothered," the elf said. "I guess I could call it the *Sheer Terror.*"

"I think you should work on a better name than that," Roveeka answered.

Pryvyd and Moshul found the ropes that were connected to the cave pulleys. The thick lines stretched from the mast of the ship to the mouth of the cave. With some strong tugs, Moshul and the band of oglodytes were able to pull the ship out of the cave and into the sunshine.

Wily looked over to see the Recluself staring back at the dark grotto as the ship drifted into the sea.

"What a horrible place," the elf muttered.

"Or rather the best place," Jayrus said as he pulled the vectrite netting off his head.

"Let's set sail back to Panthasos," Pryvyd announced to the others. "There's no time to waste."

"No," Wily said. "Stalag is too powerful with both his magic and Kestrel's machines combined. We need something else to even the field." Kestrel was already nodding in agreement. "We need to find the Eversteel Forge."

Pryvyd and Odette, who had both witnessed the same destruction in the cave mural, were left considering this.

"I think you are right," Odette said. "It may be our only chance."

"We should go back to Lumina and the royal palace," Pryvyd said. "We may never find the Eversteel Forge. How can we take that chance?"

"Hold on," Odette said. "We are the best treasure hunters the world has ever seen. Who got to the center of the Maze of the Dissolved? We did. Who plundered Graymold Manor? We did. Who found the most valuable treasure of all in Carrion Tomb?" Odette gave Wily a big grin.

"We did," Pryvyd said, unable to restrain a smile.

"We'll find the forge," Odette said. "I believe in us."

Pryvyd sighed. "Okay. But if we don't find it before sundown tomorrow, we head back to Panthasos."

"Agreed," Wily said. He turned to Kestrel. "This has nothing to do with the fact that you wanted us to do it. It just happens to be the best idea to save the kingdom."

"I will assist in any way I can," Kestrel replied with a gentle bow of his head.

"To the west!" Jayrus shouted as he gripped the wheel of the ship. "There is a world out there that needs our unzenbach."

Wily guessed that *unzenbach* was another oglodyte word for "help." He couldn't be sure of the exact translation, but by the way Jayrus had said it . . . Wily couldn't agree more.

14

DRAKESMITH ISLAND

"Turn a few degrees to the south," Kestrel said to the oglodyte who had been steering the ship for the better part of a day. "There." Kestrel, his hands no longer bound, pointed to a cloudy spot on the horizon. The webbed-handed fish creature turned the wheel, adjusting the direction of the sailing vessel.

Nearby, the Recluself was standing by the portside railing. Wily approached the elf, who was taking long, gulping breaths.

"I keep watching for the wave that will knock me into the sea," the Recluself said. "It's not coming. I know that now."

"You sound disappointed," Wily said. "You should be happy."

"It means I could have left years ago," the elf said. "I kept myself locked away for no good reason."

"You're out here now," Wily said. "That's what's important. We all wish we could change some of the choices we made in the past."

"But they're what brought us to this moment," Roveeka added, jumping into the conversation. "All we can do is learn and make better choices in the future."

The Recluself continued to stare into the distance as his ship sailed swiftly through the night.

"Wily," Kestrel said as he approached his son, "I've got something for you to roll around in your head. Once we get to Drakesmith Island, we will need to find the forge. Lucky for us, I know the riddle that holds the secret to the location. I'm curious to hear what you make of it."

"I'm listening," Wily said.

"I am too," Roveeka added, "although riddles aren't my strong suit."

Kestrel began to intone in a singsongy voice:

To Drakesmith Island you must sail,
And climb upon the dragon's tail
Beyond the earth where the dead drink milk,
One finds the grave of the pirate's ilk.
Inside you go and there you'll kneel
At the Temple's Forge of Eversteel.

One thing Wily knew about riddles was they rarely made sense on first listen. And this one was no exception. Another thing Wily knew about riddles was that the answer would come at the strangest moment and suddenly seem as clear as the gooey ooze of an amoebolith. Back in Carrion Tomb, the Skull of Many Riddles had taught him to solve them quickly, but this one was rather tough.

"I was right," Roveeka said. "I am terrible at riddles."

"I'm not sure what to make of it either," Wily said.

"You're a Gromanov," Kestrel said as he walked back toward the ship's wheel and the oglodyte steering it. "I have faith in you."

Wily let the wind blow through his curly locks. He hoped that once they reached Drakesmith Island, clues would present themselves. The choices would become clear. Yet right now, all he could do was ponder the strange meaning of the words that seemingly did not match up at all.

"One more thing," Kestrel said as he put his hand on Wily's shoulder. "You've got to start trusting me. I can see the way you look at me. I make the same face when I think there's a trap about to spring. But I'm not a danger to you."

"Why should I believe that?" Wily asked.

"Being locked away gives you a lot of time to think," Kestrel said, "about what's important and what's not. I built countless machines. Ones more amazing than Panthasos had ever seen. But I should have been building a relationship with you. I didn't realize until it was too late that you were my finest creation."

Wily stared coldly back at his father.

"I'm not made of gears and levers. You didn't make me. I just happen to be your son."

"I'm not good at sharing my feelings," Kestrel said, "but I'm trying."

Wily watched as his father returned to where the oglodyte was steering the ship. Somehow the kind and gentle words only made Wily angrier.

As DAWN CAME, an island pushed into view through the fog. Boulder-strewn hills lay on the north end of the island, while a gently sloping jungle covered the rest. A small port was located at the center of the crescent beach on the eastern shore. While not nearly as bustling as Ratgull Harbor, there were still a great many ships moored in the shallows surrounding the network of docks. Thatched-roof buildings jutted above the quilt of awning-covered markets that spread out in both directions from the town center.

"Drakesmith Island," Kestrel said as his eyes lit up with delight. "We've made it!"

"And the Eversteel Forge is hidden somewhere in those jungles," Pryvyd said. "It would take months to search every inch of it."

"I think we should start there." Odette pointed to the north, where gray plumes drifted out from the rocks into the sky. "Forges need flames. And flames make smoke."

"If it was that easy," Kestrel said, "the forge would

have been found long ago. No, the riddle must hold the answer."

"The riddle said that after sailing to Drakesmith Island," Wily clarified, "you must climb the tail of a dragon. We need to find a dragon."

"Depending on how big the dragon is, it could be hiding almost anywhere," Kestrel surmised.

"As I said before," Odette said with a sigh, "smoke leads to fire, and what breathes fire? Dragons. We should go to the north end of the island."

"That's a good point," Jayrus said as he tapped his webbed thumbs together.

Roveeka chuckled loudly to herself. Everyone turned in her direction. She laughed again before quickly silencing herself.

"Did you figure something out?" Pryvyd asked.

"No," Roveeka said. "I'm terrible at riddles. Wily knows that. I can never figure them out."

"Then what's so funny?" Odette asked.

"You know how clouds look like things in the sky? And when you're hungry every cloud looks like a snail or a maggot?"

"Not really," Odette said. "But what does that have to do with now? The sky is cloudless."

"I was just thinking how things look like other things. The island looks like a sleeping lizard dragon. See?"

Wily turned back to the island and realized Roveeka

was right. The boulder-strewn hills at one end of the island looked like the giant reptile's head, while the gentle sloping jungle on the other side looked like the body and tail of the lizard. Smoke poured out of large stone nostrils, sending gray plumes drifting over the ocean.

"And I just thought it was funny," Roveeka continued. "Because we are looking for a real dragon and the island happens to look like one too. Crazy coincidence."

"You solved the riddle, Roveeka!" Wily said, giving her slumped shoulders a pat.

"Yay for me!" Roveeka said with pride. Then, "How did I solve it?"

"Turn the ship to the south end of the island," Wily said. "The tail we are supposed to be climbing is the sloping hill through the jungle."

Wily hurried to the bow of the Recluself's ship as it glided across the smooth waters. As it moved closer to Drakesmith Island, Wily spied a buoy floating in the water with a large sign affixed to it that read STAY AWAY. VISITORS TURN BACK.

"Guess that means we won't be getting a royal welcome," Wily said to Moshul and Righteous, who were on either side of him.

"I think it would be best if we were dropped off," Kestrel said, "and the Recluself and oglodytes remained hidden in the smoke blowing off the island. The locals clearly don't want visitors."

"It's a good idea," Odette said from her perch atop a nearby wooden barrel. "Although I can't believe I'm agreeing with the Infernal King."

"I'd prefer that you didn't call me the Infernal King anymore," Kestrel said calmly. "I'm not the same man I used to be."

"'Used to be'?" Odette snapped back. "You make it sound like it's been ages. Just one year ago, you were rolling snagglecarts all over the land, kidnapping innocent people. People don't change that fast. Even the cocoon folk take longer to sprout their wings."

"Ease off," Wily said to Odette.

Both Odette and Kestrel seemed surprised by this comment.

"Are you serious?" Odette stared at Wily in disbelief. "Have the vectrite bites made you loopy? You remember who he is? Have you forgotten the twelve years you spent in Carrion Tomb because he put you there?"

"I remember!" Wily had raised his voice. All his feelings of anger, frustration, and sorrow were bumping into one another like hobgoblets scrambling to the dinner table. Then he collected himself. "But right now, arguing and fighting is not going to help."

Odette clenched her fists before looking out at the sea silently.

"Jayrus, steer us toward that deserted beach," Pryvyd requested.

Turning the wheel counterclockwise, Jayrus guided the ship through shallows dotted with kelp and coral. As the bow of the boat cut through the water, winged fish leaped from the bay and soared above the surface, their tails flapping wildly to propel them faster. As the ship got closer to the shore, the companions lowered the sail and tossed the anchor into the sea. Once the sailing vessel came to a stop, Moshul, who still had the hugtopus wrapped around his leg, used the crank on the side of the sailboat to lower the dinghy into the water below.

Climbing down a rope ladder, Wily and his fellow companions boarded the small rowboat.

"And how will you signal the boat once you're ready to leave the island?" the Recluself said.

Moshul signed to the Recluself as Pryvyd translated for him. "I can send my fireflies out to the ship. They will land on the wheel and guide you back to our waiting point on the beach."

"Wait for our signal before returning," Wily called up to Jayrus as Moshul dropped into the boat.

The mighty moss golem grabbed the oars, and it took only a few strokes of his powerful arms to pull the group to shore. As they touched down on the pink sand, Wily was pleased to discover they were not immediately bombarded by giant mosquitoes or salt boars. He looked back to see that the oglodyte crew was already raising the sails and setting back out to the sea.

It didn't take the group long to find the beginning of

a path that led up the hill through the jungle. As they climbed the slope, they were treated to a beautiful view of the Eversteel Sea. When the sun rose higher into the sky, the shallows around the island sparkled a light green that reminded Wily of the glowing flames of his old friend the Skull of Many Riddles.

Odette was bounding from rock to tree stump with an energy that Wily hadn't seen from her in quite a while. And it wasn't even early in the morning, her happiest time.

"Happy to be off the ship?" Wily asked.

With a double backflip, she landed by his side. "Actually, I'm just happy to be doing this. Exploring. Adventuring. I know that doesn't make sense, right? Everyone wants happily ever after and we kind of had it, right? But then . . . it just felt . . ." She stopped speaking.

"What?" Wily thought he knew what she was going to say but wanted to hear it anyway.

"It's not important. But what is important is figuring out what we should be looking for next."

"The next line in the riddle," Kestrel said as he came up behind them, "is 'Beyond the earth where the dead drink milk, One finds the grave of the pirate's ilk.'"

"It sounds like a cemetery where goats and cows roam," Wily said.

"My theory exactly." Kestrel pointed up the hill to an open patch of ground where headstones stood surrounded by a wooden fence.

The group picked up the pace with the hope that the forge was not far now. As they got closer, they saw that by the entrance gate was a statue of three women raising their heads to the sky. Wily didn't see any goats right then, but he could easily imagine them wandering in through the gate.

"Someplace here is the grave of the pirate's ilk," Wily said aloud.

"*Ilk*?" Roveeka asked, eyeing the inscription on a headstone.

"It means people similar to a pirate or a pirate's friend."

"How can we know what the folk buried here were like?" Roveeka asked. "All we have are names and dates. And shouldn't there be a pathway somewhere here? Like a cave or a tunnel?"

"Just start looking," Wily said to his sister as he hurried over to the nearest tombstone. Pryvyd, Righteous, and Moshul started scanning the stones in the back, while Kestrel and Odette took the ones on the sides. Wily slowly read name after name despite the fact that he really wasn't quite sure what he was looking for. Roveeka had made a very good point.

"Here's one person that was named Gustav Highbeard," Odette called out. "That sounds like he could have been pirate's ilk."

"Moshul," Pryvyd said eagerly, "check to see if it

is hollow beneath the surface. Perhaps there is a path below."

Moshul walked over to the grave where Odette was standing. He put his ear to the ground. After a moment, he lifted his head and began to sign.

Nothing down below.

Wily and the others continued searching for what seemed like the better part of an hour. The only other name that sounded remotely like a pirate was Sylvie Scarlet, and that grave did not appear to have a secret path beneath it either.

"I think we might be in the wrong place," Roveeka said.

"How can that be?" Wily asked himself aloud.

Wily took a seat on the edge of the statue and stared out at the jungle around him. *How did I get this wrong? What am I not thinking of? This is where the dead drink milk.* Or was it? He hadn't seen any cows or goats. He stood, scanning for the animals. All he saw were trees. Palm trees. Coconut trees. Banana trees. Something clicked in his head like gears interlocking.

"The coconut trees," Wily shouted to the others. "They have milk too. Coconut milk. This way!"

Before anyone could argue with him, Wily had left the cemetery and was pushing through the dense trees for the patch of coconut trees just downhill of them. The group hurried after him. The jungle opened up into a small glen where five dozen markers were buried in the earth. Each was made of the husks of coconuts.

"This isn't a graveyard for humans. It's for animals."

"The path to the forge must be here somewhere," Wily said excitedly as he ran to the nearest marker.

Righteous was flying past the graves to a rock wall covered with dangling vines. The floating arm grabbed a fistful of the green shoots and pulled them aside, revealing a cave hidden behind a curtain of hanging moss and ivy. With much excitement, everyone hurried over.

Kestrel peered inside the cave and then turned to Wily. "Do you want to take the lead?"

"Push your son into danger?" Odette said with a sneer. "How sweet."

"Not at all," Kestrel said. "He's just proven himself to be much better at spotting traps than I am."

"Well, that's true," Odette said reluctantly.

"Very true," Roveeka added. "And he's good at a lot of other stuff too."

"I don't doubt that anymore," Kestrel said with a look of what seemed to be admiration.

Wily stepped through the ivy quickly. He didn't want his companions to see that he was smiling.

15

PIRATE'S GRAVE

The cave was not a twisting tunnel or a cavernous chamber filled with secrets. There were no traps or monsters. It was a small cave, no deeper than sixty steps and barely tall enough to fit Moshul. At the end of the tunnel was a pool of murky water and a small pile of animal bones picked clean.

"It's a dead end." Kestrel kicked the dirt.

"Maybe we made a wrong turn," Roveeka said hopefully.

"But there were no turns to be made," Odette pointed out. "It was all one tunnel. No left turns. No right turns. Just straight. Straight to a dead end."

"We might have missed something along the way," Roveeka added. "Maybe there was a small offshoot that we didn't see."

"I was looking pretty carefully," Wily said. "I was

even using my fingertips to check the walls for seams. It's the best way to find the entrances to the hidden maintenance tunnels found in every proper dungeon. I didn't see or feel anything."

"But this has to be it," Roveeka said.

"Maybe there was another tunnel entrance that we didn't see," Pryvyd said. "A staircase beneath one of the graves or a trapdoor beneath a tombstone."

"What kind of animal would be a pirate's ilk?" Wily said.

"A parrot," Kestrel said.

"That sounds right to me," Pryvyd said. Even Odette was nodding slightly.

"Let's check all the tombstones for a parrot's name," Pryvyd said. "Although I imagine a parrot wouldn't have a very big grave."

The group turned back for the entrance of the cave. As they walked, Wily imagined a pirate and his parrot fighting in a great sea battle, the two standing at the wheel as the ship sank.

"Wait," Wily exclaimed. "Maybe those plots outside were not the pirate's grave the riddle was talking about."

"We were clearly supposed to go to the coconut cemetery," Roveeka reminded Wily. "Where the dead drink milk."

"I agree," Wily said. "But that might have been a different part of the riddle. The grave of the pirate's ilk might be something different."

"Go ahead, Wily," Kestrel said. "Explain."

"When a pirate meets his untimely end," Wily said, trying to focus only on the riddle of the forge, "where does it happen?"

"On an enemy pirate ship?" Roveeka said.

"Sometimes," Wily agreed. "But where would that be?"

"At sea," Odette suggested.

"That's right," Wily said. "It's rare that a pirate is buried in the ground. They would go down with the ship. The grave of the pirate's ilk is underwater."

Wily hurried back to the murky water at the end of the tunnel.

"I'm not sure this is a dead end after all."

Odette was nodding as she looked into the water.

"Well, there's only one way to find out," she said. She stepped into the pool, sucked in a big lungful of air, and dove.

An awfully long time seemed to pass before Odette came up again.

"You've got to see this," Odette said with a big smile and a shake of her long blue hair. "And you were right. This is no dead end."

Kestrel and Pryvyd both gave Wily a nod of fatherly approval. The two men realized this and turned away from each other.

Wily and the rest of his party waded into the water before diving below the surface. With his eyes open, Wily swam through the murky water toward the far wall of the cave. Just a foot below the surface was an underwater tunnel leading to a secret pool on the other side of the wall.

Wily came up for air above the secret pool. The ceiling was arched and the room was narrow. It was like a hallway that was nearly all submerged in water. Steel lanterns with glass panels hung from above, each tinted a different shade of green. The light that shone created shadows on the walls and water in a complex pattern of hexagons. Far at the other side of the hall was a set of stairs that exited the water onto a portion of stone ground.

"Let's swim for those stairs," Pryvyd said as he began to paddle in the lead.

The group made slow progress down the long corridor. Swimming was not nearly as swift as running or even walking. Righteous flew overhead, skimming an arm's length above the surface.

"Those lanterns look to be made of eversteel," Kestrel said, peering upward.

"We must be close to the forge now," Odette said with extra delight in her eyes.

Odette is right, Wily thought. *We've done what few thought possible.* Wily felt a slight tingle run down his skin. It was an electric charge of excitement that made the hairs on his arms stand on end. It even made his lips quiver. Suddenly, Wily wasn't excited anymore. He was frightened.

"We need to get out of the water!" Wily shouted. "Right now!"

"Why?" Odette yelled.

"That tingle you're feeling is caused by electric eels," Wily said. "This is a trap. I made one just like it. I called mine the Ankle Shocker. Although in this deep water, they are going to shock a lot more than ankles."

Roveeka tried climbing the outside wall of the corridor but it was too slippery. She just slid back down into the water.

"I can't," Roveeka said.

"It's too far back to get out the way we came in," Pryvyd said, looking fearful.

Wily looked up at the hanging lanterns. He could see they made a path all the way across the long hall.

"Up there," Wily shouted. "That's the way across."

Wily felt something brush past his leg below the surface. There was little time left before the eels attacked. They were preparing to charge.

"We need a toss!" Wily said, turning to Moshul.

The moss golem was already on it. He grabbed Roveeka in his hand as Odette ran up his back and did a double flip onto an emerald hanging lantern. She hung upside down as Roveeka was thrown into the air, and she caught the hobgoblet in her arms.

Wily was next. Moshul hastily tossed him up and Righteous flew up and gave him an extra nudge to reach a pale green lantern. As Wily tightened his grip, Pryvyd and Kestrel were scooped out of the water and tossed into the air. Kestrel caught onto one of the dangling lanterns and then reached out to snag Pryvyd, who'd missed his lantern.

"Moshul," Roveeka called down. "You need to get out too!"

Moshul signed up to her. *I'll be okay. Although some of my bugs might not be. Or the hugtopus.*

As he signed the last words, the water sparked with electricity. Pulses ran up and down Moshul's body, but the moss golem seemed to be unaffected by the energy.

"The poor hugtopus!" Roveeka called out.

Wily had now pulled himself up so that his feet were braced around the lantern and his hands were firmly gripping the chains holding it to the ceiling.

"We need to get to the other side of the room by swinging from lantern to lantern," he said. "It might be easy for Odette, but it will be tough for the rest of us."

Pryvyd was peering down from his lantern at the water. The electric eels were swimming in rapid circles around Moshul, smacking him with their tails, clearly not pleased with their inability to stun him.

"Wily," Pryvyd stammered, "I should never have let you come on this adventure. I want you to know that I'm sorry I haven't been able to keep you safe. I care about you." Pryvyd looked over at Kestrel, who was next to him on the same lantern. "Like a father."

"Very touching," Kestrel said. "But he already has a father that cares about him. Even if he hasn't always been there for him before."

Wily looked over at the two men, who were now eyeing him.

"Can we talk more about this later?" Wily asked. "When we are not dangling above a deadly trap."

"It seemed like the right time," Pryvyd said. "Just in case."

"Nobody is getting hurt today," Roveeka said. "If I can do this, so can all of you."

To everyone's (but Roveeka's) surprise, she made a flying leap to the neighboring lantern. Her stumpy fingers latched on tight to the next chain as it swung under her weight. Using the momentum, she leaped to the next lantern and the next.

"Whoa," Odette muttered. "I didn't know she could do that. I must be rubbing off on her."

Roveeka got to the far side of the water-filled hallway. She was now above the stone platform.

"I guess we all can be the people we want to be if we put our minds to it," Kestrel said as he took off next.

As the others followed Roveeka's path, Moshul swam the remainder of the way with the eels shocking him to no effect. The moss golem stepped out of the water, and Wily could see, to his great relief, that the hugtopus seemed to be completely unaffected by the eels. Moshul stood under the last lantern and opened his arms to catch Roveeka. Moshul gave the hobgoblet a hug as tight as the one the little octopod was giving him to let her know how glad he was that she had made it across safely.

Despite the crossing seeming treacherous, Wily discovered it was not nearly as difficult as it had appeared to be. He fell into Moshul's big hands and was put gently on the ground next to Roveeka.

"How were you so confident?" Wily asked his hobgoblet sister.

Roveeka lowered her voice to a whisper. "Sometimes pretending to be brave is the same thing as being brave."

Wily gave her a big smile and then turned to the exit of the hall. The opening ahead glowed with orange and gold. Wily took the lead and found that it opened up to a giant cavern—

and Wily and his friends were at the top of it. He was now standing on a balcony that looked out upon a magnificent sight. He moved to the edge and looked over the side. Hundreds of feet below, Wily could see a silver step pyramid. Smoke poured out from the vent at its peak. The trail of smoke was sucked away through a long metal tube built into the side of the cavern wall.

"The Eversteel Forge," Wily said. "We've found it."

16

THE STEEL TREE

"That's how the smoke seems to pour out from the nose of the dragon on the north side of the island," Kestrel said, coming up behind Wily. He pointed to the tubes in the side of the mountain. "A series of exhaust vents have been built into the island to hide the true location of the Eversteel Forge."

"Brilliant," Wily said.

"The creators of the forge were ingenious," Kestrel said, then eyed his son. "Like someone else I know."

Wily couldn't help but smile at the compliment.

"Like someone you had imprisoned," Pryvyd said with a tinge of jealousy. It was clear to Wily that the Knight of the Golden Sun was not keen on Kestrel's growing affection for him.

"They had to keep it safe," Odette said, eyeing

the pyramid, "since it's a device that would make any woman, man, or beast unstoppable."

"Which is exactly why we needed to get to it," Kestrel said to Wily. "Your mother and Panthasos are in danger, and down there is the best chance of rescuing them."

Wily looked over the lip of the balcony. A steel ladder stretched from the high platform down to the ground. He ran his fingers over the metal handles of the ladder. He could feel the strength of the metal.

"I think this ladder will be a lot sturdier than the rope ladders and bridges we've had to traverse in the past," Wily said. "It looks safe."

"So did the submerged hallway before the electric eels swam into it," Pryvyd said, giving the ladder a tug.

"Trust the boy," Kestrel said. "He knows more about constructing things than even I do. If he says it is safe, it is."

Climbing over the edge of the balcony, Wily placed his hands on either side of the ladder. He tucked the soles of his shoes on the outside of the ladder and gently released his grip. At once, he began to slide down. He had done this a thousand times back in Carrion Tomb, but here the metal was so smooth that he didn't even need to tuck his hands into his sleeves to avoid getting splinters. He reached the bottom with a thump.

As the others descended behind him, Wily looked up at the pyramid that stood before him. It was made entirely of steel, its metallic wall reflecting its surroundings perfectly. Pieces of cracked armor and broken weapons littered the floor: metal sleeves, golden swords, and steel boots were scattered before the entrance. As the light caught the outside walls of the pyramid at certain angles, Wily could see a faint rainbow pattern shine across the surface. It reminded him of how Roveeka's knives looked right after a solid polishing. Wily could see his own reflection staring back at him. His father came up behind him and patted him on the shoulder. Wily had never looked at both himself and his father at the same time. The resemblance was more pronounced than he had ever realized before.

"A magnificent sight," Kestrel said. "The stuff of legend."

"The pyramid *is* bigger than I imagined," Wily replied.

"That's not the sight I was talking about," Kestrel said, referring to the reflection of father and son together.

A booming voice called from within the pyramid: "Whether you have come here with the best intentions or the worst, I will not let you lay your hands on the Eversteel Forge."

The statement was followed by the sound of metal chains sliding against the floor. Out from the door came a pair of creatures with human torsos and snake tails where their legs would be expected to be. Wily recognized these fearsome creatures. He had seen one in

Squalor Keep during his first dungeon-raiding adventure with Odette, Righteous, Pryvyd, and Moshul. They referred to themselves as the Summoned Ones, fierce protectors of whatever area they were asked to watch over. These snakes, however, were far more intimidating than the one they had met in the Keep. This pair was dressed from head to tail in armor made of the same shiny reflective steel that the walls of the great pyramid were made of. They each held a pair of curved scimitars, spinning them in circles as they approached.

"There is only death for those that approach," the male Summoned One said, "when we stand guard."

"No weapon can pierce our armor," the other Summoned One said as she clashed her blades together. "It was burned in the fire of the forge. It is unbreakable, just like our swords."

Pryvyd made a series of quick hand signals to Odette, and in response, she stepped back to Moshul's side. Wily watched as she casually plucked a yellow mushroom off the side of his body. With a quick toss, she threw the mushroom at the Summoned Ones' tails. It exploded in a cloud of yellow smoke—which was quickly sucked away. Wily watched as the smoke was pulled up through the air to the very same vent that continued to sweep away the billowing smoke from the top of the metal pyramid.

"I'm sure that trick has worked for you in the past," the female Summoned One said, "but not this time."

"Sometimes it works," Odette said. "Sometimes not. But this time it did."

While the guardians had been distracted by the mushroom cloud, Righteous had flown right past them, slipped into a piece of discarded silver armor, and grabbed a mighty sword. Now it was ready to do battle. Righteous took on both Summoned Ones at the same time, parrying their attacks one after the next. The snake-people's scimitars hit the eversteel plating now encasing Righteous. The blows bounced off the impenetrable armor.

"This is our chance," Pryvyd said to the others. "Righteous will hold them off until we're safe."

Wily and his friends ran for the entrance of the metallic temple as Righteous intercepted the Summoned Ones.

"Stop them," the male Summoned One shouted to his fellow guard as he parried one of Righteous's swings.

The female Summoned One tried to slither toward Wily, but Righteous was too fast for her. The arm swung the eversteel blade in a figure eight, keeping her at bay.

"It's just one arm!" she screamed. "We have disposed of a dozen soldiers before with no problem."

Wily and his fellow adventurers slipped through the large open door. Inside was one room with an enormous bellow, a coal-burning fire, and an anvil twice the size of Moshul. The fire burned a bright orange with flickers of green and blue. All along the walls, suits of gleaming armor hung beside swords and shields. There was one suit of platemail armor so huge it seemed as if it had been made for a stone golem. Most striking was an elaborate metal tree with sparkling golden leaves hanging from it. It was a sight so breathtaking that it made Wily come to a complete halt.

"It's beautiful," Roveeka said.

"Glad you like my handiwork," a gruff voice called out from the other side of the room. "It'll be the last thing you lay your eyes on."

Next to the forge, a gwarf stood with a young woman twice as tall as him. Both were holding swords pulled straight from the forge.

"The Summoned One will make quick work of your arm," the gwarf said. "Until then, you will have to deal with us."

"Before we come to blows," Wily said, "can I ask one question?"

"Go ahead," the girl said, pointing the blade in his direction. "Speak before Tonguesplitter makes that all but impossible."

"You name your blade?" Roveeka said with surprise. "I do that too. Which is not so important right now."

"That tree?" Wily asked. "Did you make it for a purpose?"

"A forge that only makes blades is not worth its fire," the gwarf said. "But I have a feeling you haven't come all this way to hear about my art. I know what you want.

Same as everyone else who seeks the Eversteel Forge. Weapons."

"That may be true," Wily said. "But please hear our story before you judge us."

"We have only one goal," the old gwarf said.

"To protect the forge from outsiders," Pryvyd answered for the gwarf.

"Wrong," the gwarf replied. "We stand guard to protect the world from the forge."

"My father is right," the girl said. "An unbreakable sword is unbreakable. A weapon like that doesn't just disappear after it is put to noble use. It remains long after that. To be used by others for less noble reasons."

"Swords and shields tear people apart," the gwarf said. "The weapons I have built have done more harm than good."

"We need to save the people who we love," Wily said. "An evil cavern mage has taken over the kingdom of Panthasos. Your forge and what we can build with it is our only chance at reclaiming it."

"The mage is using the machines that I built and enchanting them with magic," Kestrel said. "The machines that were once used for evil are now an even greater threat. The only chance we have at stopping him is to use your forge to build an army of unbreakable machines to face off against them."

"I refuse," the gwarf said. "More problems, I say. It will only lead to more problems."

Wily turned to the girl. "The cavern mage Stalag is terrorizing the innocent people of Panthasos. That's what we are fighting against."

From just outside the temple, a voice called.

"Do we still have to fight this floating arm?" the male Summoned One asked. "We're getting awfully tired over here. And you just seem to be talking in there."

"Will you tell your arm to put down the sword?" the girl asked the group.

Pryvyd nodded and then shouted, "Righteous, you can come in now. We're safe."

Righteous, still mid-battle, floated backward to get a clear view inside the temple of the forge.

"We're fine," Odette insisted. "Get in here."

Satisfied, Righteous broke off from fighting with the snake people and flew inside. After a beat, the two armored Summoned Ones slithered inside.

"Holy Glothmurk!" the female Summoned One said. "That arm is relentless. I'm exhausted."

"And we've been training every day . . . ," the male Summoned One added. "For like eight hours a day. Push-ups. Stairs, sword swinging, shield lifting."

"You've got some skills," the female Summoned One said to Righteous.

Righteous tossed the sword in the air with a flip and caught it again without missing a beat.

"In fairness," the male Summoned One grumbled,

17

FROM THE FORGE

For the next eight hours, the only conversation was about construction. Large slabs of metal were pulled from the flames and handed to Moshul, who was an expert at hammering them flat. Righteous, Pryvyd, and the two Summoned Ones were in charge of cutting them into the shapes depicted on Wily's and Kestrel's blueprints. The gwarf then drilled the screw holes in the large pieces before they were dragged over to the worktables.

Odette and Roveeka were put in charge of the more difficult task of making the smaller pieces of the machines. They poured the hot steel into molds that the gwarf's daughter had created. Once the metal was cooled, Roveeka flipped the molds to reveal dozens of silver screws of various sizes.

Wily and Kestrel had the final job in the assembly

line. They were constructing the soldiers, interlocking the pieces with the screws and bolts.

"Here's the five screws you need," Kestrel said, sliding a box across the worktable.

"Actually, I need six," Wily replied. "Found a spot that needed reinforcing."

"Six it is." Kestrel nodded, throwing an extra screw into the box before handing it to his son.

"They are looking perfect so far," Kestrel remarked as he continued working on his own machine.

Wily couldn't agree more. Standing before him were a trio of shiny silver mechanical men. They were just like the gearfolk Kestrel had made during his reign as the Infernal King, only these were built with intricate mechanics inside that would not require them to be operated by rust fairies.

"With no one inside controlling them, how will they know what to do?" Pryvyd asked as he carried over a pile of precut legs. "A soldier is not like an automated rowing machine. Many actions are required of it."

"There are powerful magnets built into the armor," Kestrel said. "They will be commanded by a Master Suit. Whatever action the Master Suit performs, the other suits will copy it exactly. It will allow a single person to control an entire army. Let me show you."

Kestrel slipped on a Master Glove. He clenched his fist tightly, and as he did the three silver mechanical men did the same.

"Amazing," Pryvyd said.

"One of the advantages of being stuck in a prison cell for months is that it gives you plenty of time to think," Kestrel replied. "I came up with lots of clever ideas while I was in there."

Kestrel removed the glove and placed it next to him.

"Let me be clear about this now," Pryvyd said, picking up the glove. "You will not be the one to lead the new army of ubergearfolk."

Kestrel was taken aback. "I constructed the machines," he said. "No one would be better equipped to control them."

"Then let's hope you are as good a teacher as you are an engineer. Because I still don't trust you. I will wear the armor."

"And how will the right arms of the gearfolk be controlled?"

"Righteous will wear that piece of the armor," Pryvyd answered.

Wily looked at Kestrel, waiting to see what his response would be.

"Fair enough," Kestrel relented. "You will wear the Master Suit."

The former Infernal King returned to the task at hand. "I figure with sixty-five of these soldiers," Kestrel said, "we should be able to come out victorious even if Stalag has rebuilt every gearfolk and snagglecart I ever made."

Kestrel slid a pair of metal legs across the table to Wily.

"This is for soldier number four," Wily's father said. "Only sixty or so to go."

JUST LIKE DURING his time in Carrion Tomb, it was hard to tell how much time had passed while they were working. Wily was so focused on the task at hand that he didn't even pay attention to his grumbling stomach. It could have been a few hours or a whole day. By the time there were sixty-five metal soldiers standing in formation, Wily was so tired he could barely stand.

"They're beautiful," Kestrel said, looking at the shining army. "We make quite a team."

"Hopefully," Pryvyd said, "this will be enough to defeat the magically enhanced gearfolk."

"I don't doubt it for a moment," Kestrel said, giving his son a wink.

"I made this for you," the gwarf's daughter said as she approached Pryvyd and Righteous.

She held a new set of silver armor in her hands. There was a breast plate, leg pieces, an arm piece, and a gauntlet for Pryvyd. For Righteous, she held a silver arm piece and gauntlet.

"They lock together if you want to fight as one," she said. "Or they snap apart if you want to be independent."

"Thank you for this unexpected gift," Pryvyd said.

"Once I no longer need to wear the Master Suit, this will be my armor of choice."

"And, of course, I have a shield and sword to match," the gwarf daughter said, handing over one with an intricate design of the golden sun rising above Drakesmith Island. Righteous seemed quite pleased to get into armor made just for it and to grab the sword. The floating arm swung the sword to test its weight and balance.

"That looks just like the pattern on Pops," Roveeka said, pulling out her knife.

The gwarf hustled over to peer down at the weapon in her hand.

"Where did you get this?" he asked Roveeka.

"It was left for me in my crib by my parents," she said.

"I made these knives for my loyal assistants," the gwarf said. "A lovely couple. Hard workers. They traveled to Panthasos to help the hobgoblets that were banished to Undertown. I believe they were captured before reaching their destination. They never returned."

"Did they have a child?" Roveeka asked.

"Not when I knew them, but they were very much in love."

"Maybe they were my parents . . . ," Roveeka said with a far-off look. "What were their names?"

"Roselle and Veekam."

A big, crooked smile spread across Roveeka's face. "Their names combine to make mine."

"Let's give this army a test run," Kestrel said.

Pryvyd approached Kestrel, who was holding pieces of the Master Suit. Wily watched as Kestrel helped Pryvyd slide his arm into the metal sleeve and place the gauntlet on his fist. Once Pryvyd's legs and chest were encased, Kestrel placed the helmet over the Golden Knight's head. It was strange for Wily to watch these two very different father figures working together.

Pryvyd took a step forward, and as he did, all the eversteel gearfolk did the same. Pryvyd continued his walk toward the far side of the cavern. The metal men followed him in perfect unison.

"We're ready," Wily said.

The gwarf walked across the floor of the cavern to a long metal wall. He peered through a pair of holes cut into it.

"Before we open up the wall," the gwarf said. "We need to make sure that there's no one lurking about out there. This secret entrance must remain a secret."

After a good long look, he pulled his face away from the holes in the wall.

"The coast is clear," he said as he moved to a large lever. He pulled down on it and the entire wall began to slide. Moonlight flooded inside as the door exposed the jungle beyond.

"Quickly now," he said. "I don't want to keep it open longer than I have to."

Pryvyd marched out of the cavern, leading the ubergearfolk into the night air. Wily, Roveeka, Moshul, Odette, and Kestrel walked alongside them. Righteous soared along above. Not a moment after they were all outside, the door began to close behind them. The gwarf's daughter waved good-bye.

"Good luck," she called out.

"When you are done with the mechanical men and the world is safe once again," the father gwarf called out, "return them to me. I will put them back into the flames of the Eversteel Forge. Then they will never fall into the wrong hands."

With that last statement, the door of the mountain was sealed shut. Wily could see that the exterior wall was made of stone to perfectly match the mountain face.

"Moshul, send out your fireflies," Wily said to the moss golem, "to signal Jayrus's and the Recluself's return."

Moshul raised his arms into the air. Out from the vegetation dozens of fireflies emerged, their abdomens twinkling in the darkness. A few of the glowing insects fluttered around the hugtopus, who beamed at them happily. After a beat, they flew out over the trees.

The group began its descent of the hillside toward the beach. Wily could see night creatures scurrying away from the strange, reflective machines passing by. "Wily." Pryvyd had walked up beside him. "I just wanted to let you know that the only reason I'm so harsh on Kestrel is that I don't want to see him hurt anyone. Especially you."

"I understand," Wily replied. "And I appreciate how much you care."

Pryvyd put a gentle hand on Wily's shoulder and gave him a pat. To their amusement, the sixty-five uber-gearfolk behind them copied the very same motion, patting the air as if there were invisible shoulders there.

"And I guess I appreciate how much they care too," Wily said, gesturing to the gearfolk.

The group slowed as they got closer to the ocean. Gentle waves lapped against the empty beach.

"They should have been here by now," Kestrel said as he looked out at the Eversteel Sea.

"We only sent out the fireflies a short while ago," Pryvyd said from behind the mask of the Master Suit. "I have faith they will be here."

"Nothing we can do now but wait," Wily said, scanning the horizon.

Everyone found spots in the sand. Wily was surprised by how comfortable the cold sand felt on his back and legs. Then again, hours of constant construction near a hot forge might make anyplace feel like an overstuffed bed.

"Hurry up!" the Recluself screamed.

Wily's eyes snapped open. He must have fallen asleep without realizing it. He peered over to see Roveeka and Odette snoring. He wasn't the only one who had been tired. Wily turned his attention to the cove. The Recluself's ship was sailing right to shore.

"What are you doing?" Pryvyd shouted to the sailboat closing in on the beach. "You'll run aground!"

"We don't have time to shuttle you on the boat," Jayrus called out as he lowered the ladder. "We're being chased away from the island. We barely made it here."

The oglodyte pointed past the mouth of the cove, where another ship was sailing.

"The locals of Drakesmith Island truly do not like visitors," the Recluself said as the bow of the ship hit the sandy bottom with a loud thud. "They have swords and axes. I was scared of the waves knocking me over. Clearly, I was worried about the wrong thing."

Wily, Odette, and Kestrel ran into the sea. Roveeka sat on Moshul's shoulders as the moss golem took large strides that sent waves churning around him. Once the water was up to Wily's waist, Wily started swimming. Reaching the ladder, he began climbing to the deck. Behind him, Pryvyd was leading the eversteel gearfolk into the brine.

"They won't be able to climb fast enough," Kestrel shouted.

"Moshul," Odette called back. "Give them a lift."

Moshul grabbed a handful of the mechanical men and tossed them onto the deck.

"Be careful with them," Kestrel shouted.

"He's doing the best he can under the circumstances," Roveeka said from his shoulders.

Moshul tossed Pryvyd and the remaining gearfolk onto the deck and started to push the Recluself's ship back out to sea.

Wily glanced toward the mouth of the cove. The Drakesmith patrol ship was making very fast time. If they had a chance at all, their escape would be very narrow indeed.

18

UNEXPECTED WHEELS

"Can we get past them?" Wily asked Jayrus, who was holding the wheel of the Recluself's ship with his webbed fingers.

"Their boat is more agile than ours," the Hammock oglodyte replied. "They've been chasing us all around the island. We barely got here without being broadsided. But I'll give it my best try."

They were on a collision course with the Drakesmith Island patrol ship. Each time Jayrus turned the wheel to change direction, so too did the opposing vessel. As if crashing weren't bad enough, Wily could now see that the other ship had giant metal spikes protruding from the bow.

"We won't let you leave the island without checking your boat for eversteel contraband," the captain of the other ship shouted.

"If we have to go into battle," Kestrel said as he pulled his sword out of his sheath, "we will do what we have to do to get back to Panthasos."

"They're not doing anything wrong," Roveeka said to Kestrel and the others. "They just want to keep the world safe."

"I agree," Wily said.

"Don't be shortsighted," Kestrel countered. "Think of who we are protecting."

"We're not battling these sailors," Wily said.

Jayrus turned the Recluself's ship hard to the right. It was matched by the local guard boat.

"I don't know what else to do," the friendly oglodyte said.

Suddenly Roveeka was pointing wildly at the opposing ship.

"Look at the front!"

Wily's vision was not quite as keen as his surrogate sister's, but he could see an object crawling up the side of the ship. Wily looked harder. It was some kind of small creature with many arms. It was a hugtopus. He turned to Moshul and saw that the hugtopus was no longer on his leg.

"Your hugtopus is off," Wily told the moss golem, who looked down with surprise. "And it is on the other boat."

"It must have swum over there," Odette said. "That's a fast little gal."

"What's it doing?" Pryvyd said.

"It looks like it's evonbenning," Jayrus said with a toothy grin. "*Evonbenning* means 'surprising those you care about with a helping hand—or eight.'"

Wily watched as the hugtopus slipped onto the deck. It lifted the giant anchor and hurled it into the water. The anchor dropped into the sea with a splash, leaving a trail of chain behind it.

"I think we just got the break we needed," Odette chirped with excitement.

The Drakesmith guard ship was tugged to a halt by the anchor. The Recluself's ship zipped right past it toward the sea. The gang watched as the warriors gave chase to the little hugtopus before it jumped back into the sea.

Moshul was looking over the railing, trying to spot it. Wily glanced over too but he wasn't able to see the eight-armed creature anywhere in the water—because it was back on the deck with them.

"Wow," Wily said. "Speedy indeed."

Moshul reached out and grabbed the hugtopus, placed it up on his shoulder, and gave it a gentle pat.

"To the east," Odette said, "all the way to Ratgull Harbor."

Jayrus gave a salute and directed the ship away from Drakesmith Island. Wily turned back to take a final glance at the island that resembled a dragon. He thought about the forge that had built the gearfolk that now stood motionless on the ship, but he thought even more about the eversteel tree the gwarf had sculpted. It reminded him of the symbol he had chosen to represent the new Panthasos: metal gears interlocked with the branches of a tree. He would always strive to ensure nature and machines were working in tandem to make the world more beautiful and safer. If his mission to save Panthasos was successful, he would return to the island and ask the gwarf to mold another eversteel tree so it could be put in the palace garden as a reminder of his mission.

Soon Drakesmith disappeared from view in the night.

The ship that the Recluself had built was remarkably effective. Even still, it seemed as if the boat wasn't moving fast enough. With each swell it rode over, Wily thought about what might be happening in Panthasos. If the images he had seen on the Isle of Delight were true, then Stalag had already taken over the royal palace with the help of the enchanted gearfolk and snaggle-carts, and his mother and Valor had been taken captive to be held in the prisonaut.

Over the next night and day, the vessel sailed north of the calm waters of the Drecks, avoiding the wind-less patches that had proved so dangerous on their journey west. At one point, they passed a mysterious sailing ship drifting in circles under a perpetual thunderstorm. Odette got so excited when she saw it that she jumped onto the edge of the railing, nearly falling into the water.

"The Gale Ghost Ship," Odette called to the others.

"I've read stories of the treasures hidden in its hull. We should"—then Odette seemed to catch herself—"get back to Panthasos, of course."

She looked at it longingly as they sailed past at a distance.

"We don't need treasure anymore," Roveeka said, coming up beside her. "We have one another."

"I guess you're right," Odette replied. Yet Wily could tell she didn't quite mean it.

Hours later, the end of their seafaring journey was marked by the sight of Ratgull Harbor.

"We'll need to find an unoccupied pier to dock the ship," Pryvyd said to the Recluself.

"Actually," the elf replied, "this ship has one last trick up its sleeve. But I've never tried it before."

"Should I be frightened?" Pryvyd said.

"Only if it doesn't work," he answered.

The Recluself took the wheel from Jayrus and directed the boat to the harbor landing, where a stone ramp was used to pull ships out of the water for maintenance or to be salvaged into more buildings for the city. The Recluself pulled a lever.

The front of the ship hit the ramp—and rolled right up it!

"How is that possible?" Odette said, looking over the edge of the boat with Wily.

At the bottom of the boat were a series of wheels that were spinning rapidly.

"I was the Brine Baron's engineer," the Recluself said. "I built him some pretty amazing machines."

The Recluself's ship rumbled into the crowded shipyard. Shocked dockhands and sailors hustled out of the way as the great wooden behemoth charged through the crushed shell–covered square toward the closed gates of the shipyard.

"What is that?" Wily could hear people shout from below.

"The return of two kings," Roveeka shouted down to them.

The amphibious ship struck the metal gate of the shipyard, uprooting the fence and pulling it through town as it rolled down the narrow alleys. The Recluself had to steer carefully through the winding streets to avoid hitting the ramshackle buildings, which looked barely stable enough to stand on their own, even without being hit by a fast-moving ship.

"Turn that way," Wily called, pointing to the right. "I see an old acquaintance."

The Recluself turned the ship so that it was moving uphill toward a man in satin pants. It was the traitorous Thrush Flannigan of the *Coal Fox*, walking the grimy street with a bottle of bubbly water in hand. He looked in horrified awe at the strange wheeled ship charging toward him.

"Run him over," Kestrel whispered in Wily's ear. "For what he did to you, he deserves it."

"I have a better way of getting back at him," Wily replied as the amphibious machine rumbled closer and closer. He then whispered something into the Recluself's ear.

"Aye aye, Captain," the Recluself replied.

He spun the wheel. The ship made a hard turn on the muddy road, and the back wheel kicked up a massive spray of thick muck that splattered Thrush, coating him in a layer of grime from his well-coiffed mustache down to his painted toenails. With a look of horror, he dropped his bubbly water on the ground.

"Set sail and never come back," Wily said. "Once I retake the palace, there will be no place for you in Panthasos."

Thrush stood there speechless as a thick clump of mud fell from his hair onto the ground. "I would have done worse," Kestrel said. "You're a kinder person than I."

The ship continued up the hill, rolling past elves, gwarves, and skrovers, and straight under the cloth banner that marked the entrance to Ratgull Harbor.

"Head for the prisonaut," Wily called out to the Recluself. "We need to rescue Lumina and Valor."

Moshul directed the Recluself to steer the ship to the east along the trail they had taken many days earlier. With a turn of the wheel, the rolling ship changed direction once more and charged for the distant horizon.

"I knew it would go fast," the Recluself said with pride. "But not this fast."

The ship was traveling roughly five times the speed of a horse, far faster than it had traveled on the ocean. Driving across the plain, they passed travelers on stallions and other riding beasts as if they were standing still. Crossing through the desert, Wily looked out to see the spot where the spider tent had stood a week earlier. Now only a few postholes and some broken pots marked the spot on which it had once stood.

Farther still, they came across a town. Or at least what was left of a town. Rubble and snagglecart tracks littered the dusty ground. In one destroyed house, blocks and dolls could be seen scattered among the wooden beams and clay roof tiles. While the ship rolled past quickly, Wily's thoughts lingered on what he was seeing. *This is what all of Panthasos will look like if I don't defeat Stalag. And I don't have a lair beast to help me save the day this time. I have a different kind of beast.* He looked over at his father. *One that is trying very hard to earn my trust.*

The ship continued to follow the rough path to the east. As the afternoon sun warmed the land, the prisonaut at the foot of Mount Neb came into view.

"There are new guards marching along the walls of the prisonaut," Roveeka said, peering out with her keen night vision. "And they aren't Knights of the Golden Sun. They look like bone soldiers and boarcus."

Getting closer, Wily could see the flabby-lipped soldiers outside the gate, picking food off their tusks. The

218

living skeletons standing along the outside of the wall held their rigid poses with mindless perseverance.

"Your mom and Valor are being kept somewhere inside there," Pryvyd said, eyeing the prisonaut.

"Perhaps in the very same cottage where I was imprisoned," Kestrel nodded.

"We need to get them out," Wily said.

"Could we batter our way through?" Odette asked.

"The prisonaut is made of steel," Kestrel said. "This ship is just wood. It wouldn't be strong enough to make anything other than a dent."

"Unless . . ." Wily eyed the repaired prisonaut. The spot that had been blasted through by Stalag's spell had been patched with bolts and scraps of metal. "Unless we struck the same spot where Stalag destroyed it to free Kestrel in the first place."

"And then use the Master Suit to take out the bone soldiers," Kestrel suggested.

"I can run with Odette and Moshul for the inside," Wily said.

"That sounds like a plan to me," Odette said.

"Lower the ramp as soon as we come to a stop," Pryvyd added, gesturing to a large plank waiting at the back of the ship. "I'll get the gearfolk ready." With that, Wily's father ran into the hull of the ship, where the sixty-five suits of armor were standing in wait.

Wily pointed to the spot in the wall for the Recluself

to hit the prisonaut. The ship was moving toward it now with tremendous speed. "Okay," Wily said. "Everybody hold on tight. We are going to be hitting that wall awfully hard." He could see the guards on the tops of the walls clutching their swords as they braced for impact.

"That's the biggest snagglecart I've ever seen," one of the frightened boarcus shouted as the ship advanced.

The bow of the boat struck the weak portion of the prisonaut. Moshul was jolted so hard he was sent tumbling to the deck. The moss golem shielded his little hugtopus companion with his large mud hand as he rolled into the mast. The ship successfully broke the steel replacement piece on the prisonaut, making an opening in the wall.

On the high wall of the prisonaut, Wily saw two familiar, yet unpleasant faces looking down upon them. One belonged to Sceely and the other to Agorop.

"Yoosh are supposed to be dead," Agorop hissed through rows of sharpened teeth.

"Well, it don't matter what they supposed to be," Sceely said, elbowing Agorop. "They're not."

"Make sure they be non-living soon," Agorop called out to the bone soldiers below.

Jayrus turned to Wily. "As an oglodyte, I am deeply embarrassed to be related to these villains."

Moshul slid the ramp over the side of ship. Before it even hit the ground, Pryvyd, wearing the Master Suit, began marching the metallic soldiers down the ramp.

Righteous flew at Pryvyd's side in the final piece of the Master Suit. At once, bone soldiers came rushing toward them. Wily watched as Pryvyd pulled his sword from his sheath. Every other suit of armor followed, drawing their own blades. As the first wave of bone soldiers attacked, Pryvyd swung his sword, not to attack himself, for there was no skeleton standing before him, but to signal the other ubergearfolk to swing their swords.

Wily watched in awe as six bone soldiers were dispatched with a single coordinated swing. Bone soldiers attacked with their own swords, but they struck the eversteel armor, damaging nothing.

"This is working," Pryvyd called out in triumph.

Righteous gave a big thumbs-up to signal his approval too. As he did so, all the ubergearfolk copied his signal and raised their thumbs as well.

There was no fear or hesitation in the mechanical men. They had no feelings or thoughts; all they could do was follow commands. Pryvyd scanned the line of identical warriors, swinging and parrying against the blows coming down. Wily was awed by the sheer destructive power of these new ubergearfolk. They were even more impressive than the rolling machines that Kestrel had created. And, Wily thought, also more terrifying.

"Let's go," Odette said, pulling Wily out of his temporary stupor, "while we have the chance."

She was correct. If Valor and Lumina were imprisoned inside, there was no time to waste.

Moshul scooped up Wily and Odette, one in each hand, and lifted them over the chaos of the bone soldiers and mechanical men doing battle, putting them down at the foot of the broken wall of the prisonaut.

Odette did a double flip up and through the gap in the wall, then reached for Wily, who was slower to climb his way inside. Just on the other side of the wall a pair of boarcus stood, wielding an ax and shield.

"You're not supposed to be here," one of the two boarcus said as he swung his ax.

"Wrong," Odette said. "You're the one who's in the wrong place."

Odette did a handspring, leaping over the boarcus and tearing his shield from his fingers as she did. Before he could even turn, she spun the shield in a circle overhead and knocked him in the side of the snout. The tusk-faced guard collapsed to the ground.

His boarcus partner raised his hands in the air, dropping his weapons.

"I hate this job anyway," he said. "I just want to be a farmer. Raise some chickens. That's all."

"Is Lumina Arbus here?" Wily asked as behind him the battle between Pryvyd's ubergearfolk and the bone soldiers continued.

"All the folk from the palace are in the cottages right past the main square," the boarcus replied.

"Hand over the keys," Odette demanded.

The boarcus quickly complied. With the ring of keys in

hand, Wily and Odette ran down the cobblestone courtyard, past the fountain, to the cottages. Wily unlocked the doors and swung them wide open.

"Mom?" he shouted. He was surprised by how fast his heart was beating.

"Wily?" his mother's voice called out. "Is that you?"

Out from the darkness of the cottage, Lumina came rushing toward the door. She had shackles on her hands and wrists. As soon as she saw him, tears welled up in her eyes. "I thought I had lost you for good this time. Stalag said he had thrown you into the ocean."

"He did," Wily replied. "I very nearly drowned."

"Odette," Lumina said, giving her a hug too. "I'm so glad you are safe. Is Pryvyd . . . okay?"

Wily could hear her get choked up as she asked.

"Yes," Wily said, to which she gave a big sigh of relief. "Moshul, Roveeka, and Righteous too. We're all fine. Tired, itchy, and a bit sun-scorched but fine nonetheless."

Valor came up next with the two ferrets, Impish and Gremlin, waddling behind (with their four paws bound in chains, it made it very difficult for the little pair to walk). Wily used the keys to unlock the chains and shackles from his loved ones.

"I had a feeling that the old cavern mage wouldn't be able to get rid of you for good," Valor said with a gentle fist bump to the shoulder.

"But how did you get back here?" Lumina asked.

"It's not a short story," Wily said. "I will tell you everything on the way to the palace."

"We can't go there," Lumina replied. "Stalag's army is too powerful. We need time to prepare and get reinforcements."

"We have reinforcements. Mechanical ones. We built soldiers with the help of the Eversteel Forge. Led by Pryvyd, they can take back the palace from Stalag."

"This sounds like something I have to see," his mother replied with amazement.

Just then her eyes went wide. She pushed Wily out of the way, knocking him to the ground in her rush to face the adversary behind him on her own.

"I won't let you take him," his mother said with a fierce growl in her voice. "Not again. Not ever."

Wily turned to see that Kestrel was standing in the doorway.

"It's nice to see you too, Lumina."

Lumina picked up the chain that had only moments before been binding her and swung it in circles before her.

"Put that down," Kestrel said. "You could hurt someone."

"I *will* hurt someone. You, to be precise."

"I'm on your side now," Kestrel said.

"Very funny," she said without smiling.

"Mom," Wily said. "He helped build the machines. Stalag threw him into the ocean too."

"I don't believe it," she said with her arms crossed.

"I didn't either," Odette said. "Still don't really."

"The palace belongs to Wily," Kestrel said. "I am here to make sure it is his once more."

Lumina looked to Wily.

"We wouldn't be here without him," Wily said.

His mother appeared lost in thought for a moment, but then she seemed to come to a decision. She reached out a hand to Wily and lifted him off the floor. "Every minute we wait, Stalag has more time to transform the palace into one of his dungeons."

And with that, she wrapped her arm around her son and walked him out the door, right past Kestrel.

"We're not the only ones from the palace in here," Valor said. "Every cottage in the prisonaut is filled with people who want to see Stalag removed from the throne. We may not need to go far to get the rest of our army."

19

SWORD AND GEARS

As the doors to the prison cottages were swung open, Wily saw old friends pour out. A dozen Knights of the Golden Sun that had aided them during their search for the famed lair beast Palojax saluted the young prince upon their release. A whole kitchen's worth of hobgoblet chefs walked into the night air with their warty fists held high. Even the giant slug from Carrion Tomb slithered out of one of the cottages, lowering her eyestalks as she exited the door.

"I am going to need all of your help," Wily shouted to the crowd that was gathering in the courtyard of the prisonaut.

"As always, our loyalty lies with you," Spraved, the Knight of the Golden Sun and commander of Halberd Keep, said with a salute.

"And I'll shake and slime anyone you ask me to," the giant slug added.

"I may be the prince," Wily continued. "But I am not your ruler. It is your choice if you want to march on the royal palace."

"If you are trying to dissuade us from joining you," Valor shouted, "you're doing a bad job."

"We want to see Stalag get justice as much as you do," a familiar voice cackled out from behind the hobgoblets.

Wily turned to see the Skull of Many Riddles floating in the air, surrounded by green flames. "What's satisfying and sweet but you can't put in your mouth to eat?" Then it answered its own riddle: "Revenge." The skull let out a laugh. "I like riddles that aren't funny so much better!"

"We stand with you, Wily," Spraved shouted. "You have earned our trust."

A chorus of cheers echoed through the prisonaut's courtyard. Wily smiled, encouraged by their belief in him.

"Just be aware," Wily said, "that we will be joined by an unexpected ally. The Infernal King."

The entire gathering of prisoners murmured with confusion as Kestrel stepped into the open before them. Wily wondered if their trust had just vanished.

"Are you crazy?" a knight called out. "That tyrant will never be a friend to us."

"I'm a changed man," Kestrel called out, setting off more murmurs.

"If I can stand beside him," Wily said, "you should be able to as well."

"He's your father," someone else yelled from the crowd. "Of course you forgave him."

"Which is why it was all the harder."

There was more muttering and grumbling from the crowd.

"I said it once," Spraved said, "and I will say it again, we trust you."

"Everyone should board the ship," Lumina said in her most commanding voice. "There is an imposter in the royal palace. Our first priority is removing him. Then we will deal with the Infernal King. And deal with him we will."

That last comment got a cheer from the crowd. The crowd of freed prisoners moved past the bound boarcus, who were seated back-to-back in the courtyard of the prisonaut, and toward the great armored ship jutting through the outer wall.

Agorop and Sceely were also tied up and being led by Jayrus to the ship.

"Let us stay here in the prison," Agorop pleaded. "There be no needing to take us anywhere."

"No one is listening to your begging, you web-footed fool," Sceely snapped at him as Moshul pushed them ahead.

"And no one should," Jayrus said, tugging them along. "You two are incredibly rude and inconsiderate. I need to teach you both some manners."

As Wily walked along the cobblestoned ground he spied Pryvyd standing with Lumina. They were embracing each other tenderly.

"I was so worried about you," Lumina said.

"I should have told you months ago how I felt," Pryvyd said. "I shouldn't have waited until it was too late."

"Pryvyd," Lumina said, "now is not the time."

"No, it is exactly the time. Before battle. Before danger. Before I may never get the chance to say it again."

Pryvyd gathered up enough courage and spoke.

"I care deeply about you," the Knight of the Golden Sun said, "and I am not just saying that because the man you were once married to is standing a hundred yards away. When I was stuck on those islands, I kept thinking that if you had been there I would never have needed to leave. Although maybe not the one with the giant mosquitoes. Even if you were there it would have been pretty awful. I'm rambling now."

Lumina gave him a gentle kiss on the cheek. "I had a hunch that's how you felt about me. But it is nice to hear it nonetheless."

Wily smiled at the thought of Pryvyd and his mother together. They loved each other and he loved them both as well. It was like a tight family growing even tighter.

Valor came up behind Wily and stood alongside him. "I don't know how much more mushy stuff I can take," she said. Then she took Wily's hand. "Perhaps a little more."

This caught Wily completely off guard. He looked down at her fingers touching his. Was this some mistake? Perhaps. Because as soon as she saw him staring down at her fingers she pulled them away. Wily watched as Valor continued along, heading to the boat. Odette, Moshul, and Roveeka moved up behind Wily.

"There's a lot of kissing and hand-holding," Roveeka said from her perch on Moshul's shoulders. "But I'm not seeing a lot of hugging. I think I can change that."

Roveeka wrapped her arms tightly around the big mud golem. He gently patted her bald head with his hand. The hugtopus moved over and got in on the action too. Moshul signed: *Thanks. I needed that.* Odette put a hand on Wily's shoulder. "Mortal danger seems to make love grow stronger. Between friends and between people who are more than friends."

"What are we, then?" Wily asked.

"Family," Odette said with a smile. "One big family."

Wily felt like giving Odette a big hug. So he did. His nose was filled with the smell of slightly spoiled yams, a sticky-sweet aroma he found delightful.

"Can you believe we are still wearing pajamas?" Odette said. "I'm really looking forward to changing into a fresh pair of pants. And, by Glothmurk, you could use a clean shirt."

Wily looked down at the tattered nightshirt he was wearing, which sent the two into a fit of giggles.

"Glad both of you are in good spirits," Pryvyd said as he and Lumina came up beside them. "We'll need all the strength of spirit we can muster." Lumina was staring through the hole in the prisonaut wall. Then she scratched her head in confusion.

"Is that a sailing ship? On land? With wheels?"

"That's another long story," Wily said. "We can tell you on the way to the royal palace."

AFTER AN HOUR of traveling the crooked road known as Trumpet Pass, the Recluself's ship came to a stop just outside the orchards. Wily could see that Stalag's gear-folk and snagglecarts were stationed in a line to defend the wall of the royal palace from intruders. It was an intimidating sight. Black smoke drifted off the gearfolks' ax blades. Spears of crackling energy had been mounted on the sides of the snagglecarts, as if the machines themselves hadn't been scary enough without them. On the high tower's balcony, Stalag stood like a lone twig growing out from the stone.

"This battle will be for the freedom of all Panthasos," Odette said to Wily as she stood by his side. "And I've got to say, life was a lot easier when all I wanted to do was get away from this place rather than save it." She paused for a moment and then continued: "But who ever said life should be easy?"

Stalag, with his arms crossed, looked down at Wily and his friends. Then the mage began to speak. His words, enchanted by some deep magic, were magnified louder than thunder.

"What a precious reunion," Stalag said sarcastically. "Father and son, finally together."

"We have a common goal now," Wily shouted up to him. "Defeating you."

"After what he did to you?" Stalag laughed. "If you only knew how he told me to treat you, you wouldn't be so ready to forgive and forget."

"Don't listen to him," Kestrel said. "He's a bitter and jealous old mage."

"I followed your whims," Stalag said. "Or at least I made you think that I was."

Wily looked over at Kestrel, who was now avoiding eye contact with his son.

"He said I should never show you kindness," Stalag continued, "in order to make you weak in spirit. And to never let you eat too much because it would make you strong in body. He told me to lock you in a cage if you misbehaved or tried to escape. Even I couldn't be so cruel."

"Lies," Kestrel insisted.

Wily wondered how much of what Stalag was saying was actually true. He suspected more than Kestrel would admit.

"I don't care if you believe me," Stalag said. "I'll kill you both just the same. I'll kill you all."

"Don't be so sure," Wily said.

"I may not have stone golems this time," Stalag said, "but I have something far more potent. Machines and magic together."

"We've brought machines of our own," Wily called back. He gave a signal, and Pryvyd and Righteous, together wearing the Master Suit, came marching toward the edge of the ship, the ubergearfolk following in line behind them.

Stalag seemed unperturbed. "How fitting this will be, Kestrel," he shouted. "Your old machines against your new ones. It is like a battle against yourself. I will enjoy watching from on high. Gearfolk! Stop that"— Stalag pointed to the amphibious sailing ship—"thing, whatever it is."

"It's the *Daring*," the Recluself called out. "That's the name I have given it."

"When I take it from you, it will make a great addition to my army," Stalag said as he rubbed his fingertips together.

Dozens of snagglecarts came rolling down toward the amphibious ship. The first two dragon-shaped carts, with spears pointed forward and ready for battering, made contact with the front wheels of the *Daring* as it rolled ahead. The spears crackled with magic upon contact, but didn't stop the Recluself's ship. The force of the giant rolling vehicle crushed the snagglecarts, flattening them underfoot. Wily watched as the rust fairies fled the machines before they were flattened too. Four more snagglecarts struck the rolling boat immediately after, their spears getting imbedded in the wooden hull. Two of the enhanced snagglecarts were rolled over easily by the ship. The next two, however, got caught in the wheel wells, grinding the amphibious vehicle to a stop with an ear-piercing screech.

"They didn't break through the ship," Wily said, concerned, "but they did manage to break it."

"Wily, Pryvyd," Kestrel said. "We have only one chance at this. I know how the gearfolk were built. I know how to defeat them. Let me prove to you that I am not the man I used to be."

"Just tell me how it can be done," Pryvyd said. "I will follow your suggestions."

"I know just where to hit them below the neck," Kestrel said. "If you fail, we all fail."

Pryvyd was already shaking his head when Wily said, "Let him. I trust he will do the right thing."

Pryvyd relented. He slid off the armor and handed it to Kestrel. Righteous, however, was less keen to give in.

"Take it off," Pryvyd said.

Righteous tried to fly away, but Pryvyd caught him

and detached the plating from the hovering arm. Kestrel put the armor on and tested a swing of his sword. All the ubergearfolk followed suit.

"Let's hurry up!" Odette shouted.

"Follow my lead," Kestrel said to Lumina.

"There's no one who knows how to break what you build better than I," Lumina said, as she pulled a scarf across her face. "I've had lots of practice."

Impish and Gremlin raised their paws as if to remind Lumina they were there too. Lumina looked over to her two furry sidekicks.

"With your help, of course," Lumina said to them. "I would have just been a rogue wearing scarves without my loyal ferret saboteurs."

This made the two ferrets smile broadly.

Kestrel put the helmet of the Master Suit on his head and marched down the ramp as the army of eversteel gearfolk followed.

Kestrel and Lumina rushed into battle with the gearfolk. Lumina darted through the opposing army, leaping onto the shoulders of one of Stalag's magical mechanical minions. The gearfolk swung its enchanted ax at Wily's mother, but she was able to spin out of the way of the sharpened blade. With a series of twists, she popped off the head of the mechanical man, sending the rust fairy flitting off in terror. Impish dove into a rolling machine and with her small hands broke it apart from the inside, causing its wheels to come rolling off and its arms to snap out of place. Gremlin had a more explosive tactic, twisting the inner workings of another and causing it to explode in fits of smoke and flying gears. Magical axes were of little use to the gearfolk when they were separated from their arms.

Kestrel, meanwhile, led his army of ubergearfolk into battle with unwavering confidence. He seemed to delight in the combat, swinging his sword like the conductor of an oglodyte orchestra, every minion following commands as if their lives depended on it. Kestrel struck the old gearfolk in the armored gut, dispatching them with simple precision. Then, with a uniform kick, he knocked his former soldiers to the ground and marched over them. The rust fairies controlling Stalag's gearfolk never even got to swing their weapons.

"You should have stayed in your tomb," Kestrel called up to Stalag. "You were never destined to rule the Above."

"You think that I was your pawn?" Stalag said. "No. You were always mine. I knew that if you were taken out of the picture, this land would be mine. Don't think for a second that you were smarter than me."

"Look around you," Kestrel snorted. "Who is wise and who is not?"

Stalag clenched his brittle fists as he looked down upon his army being crushed underfoot.

Kestrel and Lumina were joined on the battlefield by the goblin chefs, the Knights of the Golden Sun, and the giant slug, who all did their part to combat the gear-folk. Even the Skull of Many Riddles was trying to bite the rust fairies out of the gearfolk armor. Despite the danger and chaos, it was a beautiful sight. Wily's friends from all through his life were joined together, working as one, as a team. They fought arm in arm even if they didn't have arms.

"How am I doing, Wily?" the giant slug said as she tossed a gearfolk across the battlefield.

"I couldn't have done it any better."

Roveeka and her fellow knife-tossing hobgoblets had seized control of a snagglecart and were driving it through the battlefield, catching gearfolk in its large metal mouth.

"Over there," commanded Roveeka, pointing to a group of metal men engaged with Spraved and the Knights of the Golden Sun.

"You got it, Grand Slouch!" A palace hobgoblet turned the snagglecart toward the knights in danger as Roveeka hopped off the top of the steel machine and onto Moshul's back.

Wily glanced up to see the growing anger on Stalag's face.

"This isn't over yet!" the cavern mage shouted as he raised his arms overhead and fired off bolts of energy at Kestrel's eversteel soldiers. The electrical jolts just bounced off harmlessly. Enraged, Stalag tossed a scorpion from the balcony, which grew in size as it flew through the air. By the time it hit the ground, it was as large as a crab dragon.

"We need to get to Stalag," Wily said. "We can't let him escape again. Once he realizes his magic won't win the day, he's going to take off on his giant cricket."

"But how do we get up to the balcony before he disappears inside the castle?" Odette asked. "Are you going to build another flying machine?"

"There's no time for that."

Wily thought back to just over a week before, when he was standing up on that balcony rather than looking at it from the ground. So much had changed since he had fallen into Moshul's waiting arms. If only he could go back to that moment—

"I can't get up there," Wily said suddenly to Odette, "but you can."

"Moshul," Wily turned to the moss golem, "you were able to catch us when we fell off the balcony. Now I need you to throw Odette back up onto it. With her gymnastic skills, she should be able to stick the landing without getting hurt."

Both Moshul and Odette were considering.

"If he threw me high enough, far enough, and with proper aim, then yes," Odette said. "But otherwise . . ."

Moshul began signing. *I feel a whole lot better about catching people than throwing them.*

"You've got the best knife tosser sitting on your

shoulder," Wily said. "She can teach you how to throw. But you don't have a lot of time for practice."

The giant scorpion was attempting to crush the ever-steel soldiers in its pincers, but Kestrel's army's armor was too powerful. They fearlessly marched forward as the stinger tried to stab them. There was no need for them to dodge or have quick reflexes; they were impenetrable.

It was practice time for Moshul. The moss golem picked up a fallen gearfolk and tossed it underhand toward the balcony. The suit of armor flew upward, looking, at first, like it was heading in the proper direction before missing the balcony and smacking against the wall. It dropped down, hitting the rocks at the edge of the moat with a sickening thud.

"Maybe this isn't such a good idea after all," Odette said.

"You can't throw it underhand," Roveeka said. "You won't get enough control. Try overhand instead."

The mud golem nodded.

"You'll get it this time," the hobgoblet encouraged him.

He picked up the next gearfolk and this time threw overhand. The suit of armor smashed hard into a high portion of the wall before crashing below.

"Huh," Roveeka said. "That technique always works for me when I'm throwing knives."

"She's not a knife," Pryvyd shouted as he realized what was about to happen. "Wily, we've got to try something else. I'm not letting her get hurt. Send me instead."

Odette pushed Pryvyd out of the way, grabbing a sword from the ground. "No way. This is my turn to be the big hero. I know that. Throw me, Moshul!"

Moshul picked Odette up and launched her into the sky. Wily wasn't sure if it was Moshul's aim or the way in which Odette positioned her body, but the elf soared like an arrow (or perhaps like a well-balanced knife) straight for the balcony. Wily watched as Odette caught the edge of the stone railing and vaulted herself up onto the balcony. Even from this distance, Wily could tell that Stalag was so startled to see her that he nearly stumbled off the side. She pointed her sword at the frail wizard's chest.

Stalag raised his hand and shouted down below. "Rust fairies, put down your weapons. I surrender!"

The rust fairies zipped out of the suits of armor and fled into the sky. All the gearfolk fell to the ground limp and lifeless. The goblin chefs cheered as the Knights of the Golden Sun raised their arms in celebration.

"The king shall take his seat on the throne again," Pryvyd cried.

"Yes, I will," Kestrel said. Then he spun around and smashed Pryvyd over the head with the blunt end of his sword.

20

THE BATTLE OF KINGS

Pryvyd dropped to his knees. Righteous zipped to his aid, but another quick blow from Kestrel's sword knocked the hovering arm into the metal cage of an open snagglecart.

Kestrel turned to face Wily. As he did, all the other metal soldiers did the same.

"So all this was so you could take the throne again?" Wily asked. He was seething. All his worst fears about his father had been justified.

"Don't think about it like that," Kestrel said. "We both wanted the same thing: for Stalag to be removed from the palace."

"Not like this," Wily said.

"I asked you once to join me," his father said. "I will offer it again. We could rule Panthasos together, in a fair and just way. There is nothing wrong with order."

"Order at the expense of freedom is enslavement," Wily said. "The Infernal King will never take the throne again. I would never be a part of that."

"Unfortunately for you," Kestrel said, "I am in control of this army. And, in time, I will build hundreds more gearfolk. They say one man is not an army, but in this case, I am."

"You will not get away with this," Lumina said to her former husband. "We will not let you take back the land."

"I learned a lot from my failure with the last batch of gearfolk," Kestrel said. "Watching you disarm them and break them to pieces has taught me a tremendous amount. And these new mechanical men have none of the same weak points. I saw to that. With the help of our brilliant son."

Impish and Gremlin bounded to the nearest magnetic mechanical man. Kestrel swatted his hand, batting the ferrets away as if swiping at a pair of flies. "Your ferrets should crawl back into a hole and nibble nuts instead. They won't have much luck trying to blow up the unbreakable armor from the Eversteel Forge."

"Together we can bring them down," Valor shouted as she leaped into battle with Roveeka and a troop of goblin chefs. Kestrel merely laughed. He started swinging his blades, creating a wall of swinging swords so tight that even the thinnest elf couldn't squeeze through.

"It's no use," Wily said. "I built every one of those

with him. Claws and butcher knives will do nothing. But I know something that will."

Wily reached into his boot and from it pulled a single screwdriver.

"Surrender," Wily said to Kestrel, brandishing the tiny tool.

"How adorable! A hero to the very last," Kestrel scoffed. "But unless that screwdriver has been enchanted by magic given to you by the all-powerful Glothmurk herself, I'm not worried."

But Wily wasn't listening. Instead, he lunged at his father. Kestrel swung his sword, and Wily ducked in the nick of time, the blade just missing the top of his head. Wily pulled off a roll that he thought Odette would be proud of and ended up kneeling before Kestrel, who stabbed down again with his sword, slicing the trapsmith belt right off Wily's waist.

Wily desperately scanned the suit of eversteel armor, waiting for the right moment to strike his target. Just below the breastplate on the right torso was a thumb-size screw. It looked no different than the five other screws lining the chest portion of the armor. But Wily knew it was. His arm shot out, and the end of the screwdriver stuck straight into the small indentation. With a twist of his wrist, he spun the screw fast and hard. In a flash, it popped out of the suit of armor and fell to the ground.

Kestrel looked down and let out a laugh. "Only a thousand more to go."

"Nope," Wily said. "All I needed was one."

And he was right: all of a sudden, dozens of identical screws popped out of the eversteel soldiers.

"I have no idea what you're planning, but this ends here," Kestrel said, and lifted his sword into the air.

As he did so, his armor split apart. It was as if every piece of metal had been locked together by a single screw. Kestrel was left standing in his pants and tunic, with only his gauntlets left on his hands. Nearby, the eversteel soldiers were collapsing. Each was falling into a pile of unbreakable scraps.

"What have you done?" Kestrel screamed in anger.

"That sixth screw I added to the design was built in as a precaution. Just in case something like this happened. Actually, because I was expecting something like this to happen."

"What happened to giving second chances?" Roveeka said. "I thought everyone deserved one."

"They do," Wily said. "But Kestrel has had far more than two."

"You deceptive little creep," Kestrel said as he took steps backward. "You tricked me. Maybe you are more like me than I thought."

"Being prepared isn't being deceptive," Wily said. "And I am nothing like you."

Kestrel dropped his sword, turned, and began sprinting for the palace drawbridge.

"Cut him off before he gets away," Lumina shouted to Valor.

Valor, riding on the back of her mount, Stalkeer, sped forward and bounded between the former Infernal King and the lowered drawbridge. But it suddenly became quite clear that wasn't where Kestrel was heading. The former resident of the royal palace sprinted up to a large boulder in the ground. He jammed his finger into an indentation in the stone and tapped quickly on it in a very specific pattern that Wily couldn't see. A secret door in the boulder slid open.

"Where did that come from?" Lumina said. "I didn't know that was there."

Kestrel had lived in the palace since he was a little kid. It was no surprise he knew of more secret exits and entrances than Wily and his mom. As Kestrel disappeared into the darkness beyond the door, he hit a button on the inside wall to close the door once more. Wily knew that if he didn't get there fast and soon, the secret door would slam shut and he would have a very tough time opening it again. He scooped up Kestrel's fallen sword and took off.

He had to reach it before it closed. His feet flew fast, but judging by his speed and the distance, he wasn't going to make it. He needed to go faster. Still, his legs weren't as quick as Valor's. It appeared he was out of luck. Just then, something flew over his shoulder. It was

Pops, Roveeka's knife. It stuck into the doorjamb, blocking the door from fully closing. The mechanics of the door struggled to push the blade. The extra second was enough time for Wily to slip through. As soon as he was inside, the secret door smashed closed, knocking Pops to the ground outside.

It was dark inside this secret tunnel. He could hear his father running away. Wily gave chase. His feet pounded against the floor. He had no time to worry about where he was heading and what might lie beneath his feet or before him. All he knew was that he had to stop his father, once and for all.

Suddenly the hall opened up into a large square room that was as wide as four dining halls and equally as long. Square tiles covered the floor in a checkerboard pattern of green and gold. Magical torches dimly illuminated the space. The walls and ceilings were dotted with holes and slits through which Wily could only imagine what might pop out. Looking across, Wily could see that Kestrel was already at the other side of the room.

"You know what this is?" Kestrel said with an eerie calm. "My masterpiece. The ultimate trap room. A room that is impossible to pass for anyone without the knowledge buried in my head."

Wily looked hesitantly at the floor ahead. Kestrel stood smiling and gloating.

"I've been through this room hundreds if not thousands of times. I know every step by heart. You . . . not so much. Swinging hammers, darts, dropping spikes, even a bottomless pit. This room has them all."

Wily's eyes darted around the huge space. He could see where the attacks would come from, but he had no idea what would trigger them.

"I see you looking, but there are no maintenance tunnels here to sneak through. Good luck making it even a few steps. You'll perish like everyone else who has ever tried."

"You can't scare me," Wily said, pulling Kestrel's sword from its sheath, but inside, he was despairing. Without knowing the pattern, it would take him hours to traverse the floor if he didn't want to get himself killed.

Then he noticed that the floor was filthy. This was good. Cleaning was an essential part of good trapsmithing. From a dirty floor, valuable information could be inferred. He eyed the room for footprints, and sure enough, a path led through the room.

"With nobody to clean up," Wily said, "traps are much less effective. You left the safe path for me to see."

He started to bounce from stone to stone in the same pattern as Kestrel. He skipped past the holes in the wall that would shoot the poison blowgun darts. He moved past the hidden turrets caked with ashy residue that would blast fire and he slipped under the spikes that would drop from above without a single one triggering. Each step was carefully made on one of the tiles with a footprint already on it.

Then Wily placed his left foot on a tile with one of Kestrel's shoe marks, and he heard a *click* and a *whoosh* from above. A sharp spike thrust downward. Wily dodged to the left, but the serrated tip jabbed into his shoulder, knocking him to the floor and leaving a nasty gash.

"Come, now," Kestrel said. "You didn't think I'd leave you a completely safe trail, did you? I knew what kind of tricks you would be up to. I know how you think."

"You are more evil than I ever could have imagined," Wily said.

"Foolish boy," Kestrel said. "I was the Infernal King. And I still am. It's time to finish you. You've proven to be more of a threat than I thought. But I thank you for helping me defeat Stalag. He was always waiting to take my place."

Kestrel leaped from tile to tile, pouncing on Wily before he was able to stand. He grabbed Wily by the shoulder, digging his thumb into the open gash and knocking his weapon away.

"I really wish you had stayed in the tomb just like Stalag," he said as he lifted up his sword. "You were so much safer there, and I wouldn't have had to kill you."

Wily reached out, but not to grab his weapon, which was too far away to reach. Instead, he slammed his fist down on a nearby tile, sending another spike dropping. Kestrel had to dodge backward to avoid being smashed by it.

"What are you doing?" Wily's father said. "You'll kill yourself."

"And you in the process," Wily replied. "I'm not giving up without a fight."

Wily slid backward, elbowing hard another pressure plate. A jet of fire shot forth, singeing the arm of his father. Another roll backward sent darts flying and large stones falling from the ceiling. Wily dodged to the side, hitting the button that sent half the floor falling into the abyss of a bottomless hole.

Kestrel was now balancing on the edge of the pit, just like Wily. Kestrel tried to regain his footing, careful not to step on a green pressure plate near his foot.

"Move again, and you will die to regret it," Kestrel said.

Wily eyed the green pressure plate his father was trying to avoid. He knew that meant he had to do whatever he could do to press down on that stone.

"Reconsider your choices, son," Kestrel said. "We are family, whether you like it or not."

"I chose my own family. And you're not part of it."

Wily rolled across the floor, setting off blasts of icy air and dropping toxic slime onto the tiles. He reached the spot where one of the fallen stones had landed. He picked it up and tossed it toward the green pressure plate.

"No!" Kestrel shouted as he searched for a place to hide.

With a thump, the stone landed on the pressure plate that Kestrel had been making sure to avoid. A swinging hammer dropped from the ceiling. The head of the hammer hit Kestrel in the chest and knocked him off his feet and toward the bottomless abyss. The Infernal King flailed in midair as he tried to catch onto something before dropping into the hole. His fingers caught hold of the rocky edge of the pit.

"Help me," Kestrel said.

Wily had only a moment to consider. *Should I let my father die the way he would let me die? Or am I better than that?*

Wily ran for his father, following in his dusty footprints. He jumped from tile to tile. He was about to step on a shiny gold plate when—

"No," Kestrel cried. "Don't step there! That was another trap I had set for you!"

But it was too late: Wily's momentum carried him onto the gold plate before he could stop himself. As he did so, an enormous rolling boulder dropped from the ceiling. Wily was able to fall backward just before it struck him. But the boulder kept rolling—straight for his father. The Infernal King tried to move to the side, but there was nowhere to go. It struck him in the chest and sent him tumbling into the abyss.

21

TRAPLESS TREASURE

The Recluself's ship glided swiftly across the ocean, passing Oris Rock, its large stone head sticking out from the water. Stalag sat on deck, bound in enchanted shackles, peering fearfully at the Salt Isle in the distance.

"You can't do this to me," Stalag pleaded. "I'm not the true villain in all this. Kestrel was. Let me stay in the prisonaut instead."

"You had us dumped out here," Wily said as he paced along the railing. "Now it's your turn to see what that's like. You can make friends with the salt boars."

Valor was leaning up against Stalkeer with a satisfied grin on her face.

"You deserve much worse," she said.

Lumina steered the ship closer to the island. As they passed near the beach, the trees began to wail.

"Even from all the way out here," Odette said, "that sounds awful. Just wait until you get right next to them."

"Take these off," Stalag wailed, his eyes quivering inside his pale skull. "I'm defenseless without my magic."

"I'm sure you'll figure out some way to survive," Wily retorted. "Just like I had to all those years in Carrion Tomb. Word of advice: stay away from the horsetrap plants."

"Please . . ." Stalag begged. "Spare me. I burn so easily in the sun. And I can't swim."

"You're enjoying this, aren't you?" Odette asked Wily.

"So much," Wily replied.

The amphibious ship pulled up onto the shore of one of the Salt Isles, the metal bow grinding against the bottom of the salt crystal beach.

"You can't leave me here alone!"

"Okay," Wily said. "If you insist. We won't."

Pryvyd came out of the hold leading Sceely and Agorop, also bound in enchanted chains.

"You got shavtibured too?" Sceely asked. (*Shavtibur* is one the many words that oglodytes have for "ambush." This particular word means "to be captured with no hope of ever escaping.")

"I think it won't be all bad," Agorop said. "We can make a little fungus farm and I will sing you to sleep every night."

If Stalag was upset before, now he was practically

crying. The cavern mage clutched at Wily's ankle. "I'd rather be alone. Put them on a different island."

"That's insul-ter-ating," Agorop said.

Moshul lifted Stalag up by the back of his cloak and tossed him into the shallow water. Then Moshul tossed Agorop and Sceely as well. Wily reversed the oars as Stalag held his shackled hands up in the air.

"No! Come back!" Stalag called as the two fish-headed oglodytes paddled to shore with their ankles bound.

Wily didn't even look back. If he never saw Stalag again, he would have no regrets. Pryvyd walked up beside him.

"Stalag's been caught," the knight said. "Kestrel is gone forever. What now?"

"We return the ubergearfolk to the keeper of the Eversteel Forge," Wily said. "I thought he could make something else in place of these mechanical warriors."

"You have something particular in mind?" Pryvyd asked.

"I was wondering if he could make a mechanical flying machine," Wily said. "Just like the one we built ourselves, only much bigger and much stronger."

"So we could all take a ride?" Roveeka asked. "Just like a birk!"

"Or steel aqueducts. Or a forest of eversteel trees. Anything but weapons and shields."

Lumina walked up to Pryvyd's side.

"There's something I wanted to talk to you about," Lumina said.

"If this is about letting Wily jump out the window," Pryvyd said, "I just wanted to say I will never let it happen again."

"It wasn't going to be about that . . . but it is now. When did this happen?"

Pryvyd seemed to regret opening his mouth about that last bit. He quickly changed the subject.

"So what did you actually want to talk to me about?" he said swiftly.

"Before going into battle," Wily's mother said, "you told me how you felt about me."

"It might have been the panic of the situation . . . ," Pryvyd said awkwardly, "or the almost certain death."

Lumina was not listening to Pryvyd's nervous rambling. She was bending down on a single knee.

"Pryvyd, by the light of the Golden Sun and the arms that reach from it, would you accept a life of adventure with me?"

The Knight of the Golden Sun seemed dumbfounded, not prepared for this.

Lumina continued, "Would you marry me?"

The words got lost in his mouth. Then he turned to Wily.

"If it would be okay with you . . ." Pryvyd asked.

A huge smiled formed on Wily's face. "You would be

the best dad I ever had. Although, considering my previous fathers, it's not much of a competition."

Pryvyd bent down on one knee too and pressed his cheek against the back of Lumina's hand.

"There is nothing that I could want more in the Above, the Below, or anywhere in between," Pryvyd said.

She lifted him to his feet and wrapped her arms around him tightly. Wily walked over to Odette, who stood near the railing, her blue hair fluttering in the wind.

"You know all this is because of you," Wily said.

"What do you mean?" she said.

"If you hadn't led Moshul and Pryvyd into Carrion Tomb, I'd still be there. You changed the world. And changed my life for the better."

"Being awesome is my job," Odette said. "I'm used to it. But thanks."

Wily and Odette looked over to see Moshul petting his hugtopus. He noticed that the eight-armed creature had certainly gotten bigger in the last few days.

"I wonder how large that thing gets?" Wily asked.

"I've heard some can grow to the size of a small dragon," Odette said.

"Should we tell Moshul?"

"Nah. Let him worry about that later."

"So what's next for you?" Wily asked Odette.

"I know I promised I would teach you how to read,

but there is something else I would like to do. Search for treasure."

"But you have no need for money," Wily said. "The palace treasury is overflowing with gold."

"It's not that. I miss the adventure."

"I understand," Wily said. And he did.

Wily walked over and sat down next to Roveeka, who was back to carving. As he took a seat next to her, she handed him a piece of driftwood. It looked remarkably like a bird.

"Wow," Wily said. "This is great."

"I keep getting better."

"Roveeka, I don't tell you often enough how glad I am that you left the tomb with me."

"You don't have to tell me," she said. "But I still like to hear it."

Roveeka gave Wily a playful nudge in the ribs as the Recluself's ship cut across the sea.

"Turn the ship!" Odette started to yell with excitement. "Turn it!"

Odette was pointing at a spot in the sea. Sticking out of the water was the top of a marble temple with a giant golden conch shell on top.

"It's the Lost Temple of the Brine Queen!" she exclaimed. "It only comes out of the sea once every thirty years. We need to sail there now! This is a once-in-a-lifetime find. The Sacred Eye of the Seahorse lies waiting in the final chamber."

"Is that the one that can control the winds?" Pryvyd asked.

Odette nodded enthusiastically.

"Let's really think about this," Wily said to Odette and Pryvyd. "Where there's treasure, there are traps. I'm done with all that."

Wily looked at the dungeon rising up from the sea. The pearly marble gate glistened in the sun. Beyond it was the entrance to a dark corridor. Even from this distance, he could hear strange sounds gurgling from within. It was scary and spooky . . . and enticing.

"One more dungeon," Wily said. "Then I'm done."

"Yes," Odette said. "Just one more. And maybe one more after that."

Wily adjusted his new trapsmith belt, running his fingers along the tools that were dangling from it.

"Pryvyd, change direction," he said. "Our greatest adventure awaits!"

ACKNOWLEDGMENTS

As WILY SAILS off into the distance, it's time to say good-bye to the Snared trilogy and all those who have accompanied me on this amazing journey. Before thanking the non-fiction folk, I would like express my gratitude to the characters of Panthasos who have become real over the course of the last four years. I will deeply miss the company of Odette, Roveeka, Moshul, Pryvyd, and Righteous and the dark evenings we all spent together in my office. Without the lies and cruelty of Stalag and the Infernal King, these three books would have been truly dull. And a huge shout-out to Wily, who pushed me through those long writing sessions when sleep often felt like an easier path.

Now I must thank the flesh-and-blood folk without whom I would still be lost in the very first dungeon. My editors, John Morgan and Nicole Otto, have traveled with me side by side as I explored Panthasos, guiding me through the wilds of publishing. Iacopo Bruno's stunning covers are works of art that deserve to be hung in museums. Natalie C. Sousa's elegant design has not gone unnoticed by myself, librarians, and booksellers alike. Madison Furr and Mary Van Akin have helped to spread the word about the trilogy. To the copy editors who pulled out their magnifying glasses and fine-tuned every detail. Thanks to the Macmillan Squarefish team for printing and marketing the paperbacks. And a huge thank-you to Erin Stein, editor-in-chief of Imprint. Erin, your imprint is filled with caring and supportive people because of your leadership.

Wily's adventures may have come to an end on the page, but it's looking like the trapsmith of Carrion Tomb will have a new place to shine. A giant thanks to Sheila Stepanek and Allison Milgard of Happy Street Entertainment for leading the charge to bring Snared to the small screen. I am so thankful for your vision and passion. Together, we will be making something truly special.

I want to thank Markus Hoffmann, my agent of twelve (!) years, without whom I would not have a single book to my name, let alone the shelf of hardcovers and paperbacks that I have now. You have changed my life profoundly, and for that I am forever indebted.

To Olive, who was just a kindergartener when this adventure began and doesn't remember a time before Snared. As crafty as Wily is, you are far more so!

To Penny, I will always treasure the evenings I read

these three books to you. As my first listener, you gave me both advice and encouragement from the beginning.

And to Jane, I love you more than a trapsmith loves his tool belt. While the *very* best may not have come yet, *now* is pretty darn amazing.